The Magic

The Magic Kingdom

Cathie Bartlam

Scripture Union
130 City Road, London EC1V 2NJ.

By the same author
Maggie Magpie
Operation Sandy
Tricky Business
Greenlands Adventure
Stranded!

First published 1993

ISBN 0 86201 812 9

British Library Cataloguing-in-Publication Data.
A catalogue record for this book is available from the British Library.

Phototypeset by Intype, London
Printed and bound in Great Britain by Cox and Wyman Ltd, Reading

Chapter One

Mum rushed to the door as soon as Emma arrived home from school. Emma was frozen to death and too wet and miserable from the lashing sleet, hammering down from the leaden sky, to take any notice. She hated the walk home from school, especially on days like today, and to make matters worse old Hodges had given them extra French homework tonight.

'Emma, you'll never believe it, never!'

'Believe what?' replied Emma, throwing her sodden bag on the floor and flinging her wet anorak vaguely in the direction of the radiator. Missed.

'We're *all* going! *All* of us! I thought, maybe Danny, but all of us! I can't believe it!' Mum hugged Emma, who stared at her as if she had gone mad.

'Going where?' said Emma, pulling away. She was nearly as tall as Mum and a lot stronger. Surely not another pathetic play at Danny's school, or some stupid fundraising event for CF again.

Mum dragged her to the kitchen and pointed to the table.

'Look! The envelope! *All* of us. Open it.' Mum paused. 'Hang on a minute and dry your hands.'

Emma opened the letter and stared. Four long white

slips of paper with red and blue writing and numbers and dates. She had never seen anything like this before. As she started to read, a chill crept over her, her heart seemed to slow down and the only things in the world were the tickets in front of her.

Passenger ticket, baggage check and holiday itinerary. Passenger name: Emma Fisher. Carrier: Britannia Airways. Outward journey Flight No. BY 495A. Date: June 5th. Time: 10.15. Accommodation: Concord Apartment, Orlando.

'Where's Concord?'

Mum pointed to the local travel agent's stamp and the words above it: 'Florida Fun.'

'No! It can't be. Not . . .'

'Yes, Disneyworld, Orlando. Isn't it marvellous? I never thought, what with Dad on short time, and Danny in and out of hospital, and . . .'

But Emma was not listening. She was going to Florida! Two whole weeks! They were all going. Mum, Dad, Danny and her. It couldn't be true.

'And they've got us a ground floor apartment for the wheelchair and they say we'll be able to manage fine,' Mum carried on.

'But how did we get it?' Emma was puzzled. 'You're always saying we're broke. You even said I couldn't have new shoes for school for a few weeks.'

Mum smiled and ran her long thin hands through her straight brown hair. Emma noticed that she could almost see the bones sticking through the pale skin.

'It's a gift,' she said simply.

'A gift?' Emma did not understand. 'You don't get given holidays.'

'Well, we have. It's St. Jude's. You know, the church.

Irene Watkins who helps me with the playgroup asked ages ago if I'd thought of getting Danny on one of those trips to Disneyworld, for disabled children.'

'Yes, you said.'

'Well, of course, it was out of the question. Anyway, you'll never believe it . . .'

That, thought Emma, is about the tenth thing I won't believe today.

'But they've collected enough money to send us all. And there's enough left over for spends. It's amazing.' Mum sank into a chair and looked at Emma. 'I still can't believe it.'

Neither could Emma. They must have collected money for months at the church. It was not as if anyone was rich at St. Jude's. The church, an ugly, flat, brick building, did not even have a tower or spire. It was right in the middle of the estate by the shops and had been built about forty years ago at the same time as the council houses. Emma had gone there to playgroup, where Mum still worked three times a week. She had tried and rejected Brownies, went to the Youth Club if her friends were going, and had occasionally gone to church proper with Mum on Sunday. Danny went much more than she did and Dad never went near the place.

And yet somehow these people had secretly saved up to send their family on holiday. Not any old trip either! But Florida! In a plane! No-one on their estate went to Florida. Even Irene Watkins had only been as far as Tenerife, and bossy Justine in Emma's class only managed camping in France. The rest were lucky to get a week in Wales or on the South Coast. With Dad being laid off from the factory so much, the Fishers had not been anywhere for ages.

'I've got some books and things.' Mum sprang into action and pulled a carrier bag out of the vegetable rack. Wonderful, thick, glossy holiday magazines and brochures spilled onto the table just asking to be devoured. 'Dad's going to the library on the way home. Thought we would celebrate with fish and chips.'

'From the library?' laughed Emma.

Mum playfully ruffled her daughter's thick, dark-blond hair. It was starting to dry now and curls were springing up at wild angles all over her head. Her blue eyes gleamed with happiness and it did not even matter any more that she had got a monstrous spot on the side of her nose, like a volcano peak, surrounded by mountains of freckles.

'Does Danny know?' she asked, kicking off her damp shoes as she dived into the first brochure.

'No, remember he's on that trip to a museum. I couldn't get hold of him. They'll drop him off soon.'

Danny went to a special school and got a lift there and back in a sort of converted minibus that coped with his fold-up wheelchair. He hated leaving ordinary school but after the last bout in hospital he was always tired and could not keep up with the other children. At least at the 'Special' he had made friends, and they did some of his physio for him, which gave Mum a break.

'He'll be amazed. Hey, Mum, it says here the apartment's got two bathrooms. Two! And a dishwasher. And a microwave.'

Mum made a pot of tea which sat unnoticed on the table between them as they pored over the brochures.

'Can we go to Disneyworld? It's an awful lot of dollars.'

'I told you, it's all taken care of,' said Mum. 'I must

say I fancy Sea World myself and your Dad will love the Kennedy Space Center.'

'There's this Epcot place. What's that? And some studios. Perhaps I'll be on telly. And do you think I'll throw up on the plane? Irene Watkins's niece did. And I'll need some clothes. It's eighty to ninety degrees, it says here, and my T-shirts are too small. And, Mum, don't forget suntan cream. I'll frizzle. Do you think Dad will wear shorts? There's a photo here of a really old bloke in purple and green ones.'

'Emma, slow down, love. It's three months yet. Loads of time to get ready.'

They fell silent, lost in their own thoughts. Emma glanced out of the steamed-up kitchen window. Nearly black outside, the sleet still drumming its incessant rhythm on the glass. She could hear the heavy 'flap, flap' of the tarpaulin that covered half their roof, as it moved in the strong wind. The council must be mad to re-roof the houses in their road in February. She was fed up of bumping into scaffolding and piles of tiles and it was nearly impossible to push Danny along the paths by their road.

Like a magnet the brochures drew her back to their magic spell. Brilliant blue skies, sunshine, people laughing in unnaturally-blue swimming pools, wonderful fairy castles, Mickey Mouse, and she was going to see it all. Emma Fisher, aged twelve, was going on the holiday of a lifetime. All the pictures in the brochures were true. She would slide down those water chutes, see those shows, feel the hot sun on her face, visit all the places she had never dared to dream of. It was going to come true.

Emma jumped up and ran upstairs. She was so

excited that she did not know what to do. As she peeled off her soggy school uniform she hugged her arms round her strong, powerful body, trying to hold all the happiness in, but she could not. Still in her underwear, she bounced on the bed and then rolled head over heels along the floor, crushing her discarded clothes.

I'm going to Florida! Florida! went through her head like a persistent jingle.

Downstairs the doorbell rang. Danny staggered in, looking like a skeleton even in his padded coat and wide, blue jeans.

'He's a bit puffed,' said Mrs P. his helper, handing Mum the wheelchair. 'Better watch his chest . . . the weather, you know.'

'We're going to Disneyworld!' screeched Emma, jumping down the stairs. She picked her brother up and swung him round. 'Do you hear? Florida! A plane. In June.'

'Em, be careful,' said Mrs P. grinning. They all started talking at once until Mrs P. left to get back to her minibus.

Danny sat there on the stairs. His blond hair tufted up like a donkey's mane with gel, and his pale, blue eyes, looking as if they had just been washed, darting from Mum to Emma.

'It's true, Danny Fisher. We're all going on holiday. Now, come on, time for your physio before tea.'

While Mum worked on his chest, getting him to cough up thick, gooey gunge, she told Danny all about the holiday. It was really odd, thought Emma, as she watched her brother's skinny body taking its usual pounding, that he did not ask why they were going. Why had the church given them all the money? He did not seem to realise it was because he was ill. He never seemed to realise anything, even Mum working away at his chest, was because of his cystic fibrosis. He never usually talked about it.

'What if I'm in hospital?' he said, yawning.

'Well, we'll pray you won't be,' said Mum, who always looked on the bright side. 'I'm sure a God who can give us a holiday, can keep you infection free in June. Aren't you?'

'Course.'

Dad arrived home then, fish and chips and library books mixed up together. They had a wonderful evening reading all about Florida. Emma went to bed the happiest she had ever felt in her life. Even the thought that she had forgotten to do Hodges' rotten homework did not bother her. Florida! Wow!

Chapter Two

June the fifth! At last! Emma had been too excited to sleep. The minutes on the clock radio changed so slowly that she thought it would never be time to get up. At six she was dressed and ready. Mum was working on Danny's chest while Dad went round locking everything up. Within an hour the taxi, black and important-looking, had arrived.

As they sped through the quiet streets to the airport, Emma wanted to sing aloud. She looked at the driver. Grim-faced, un-smiling, just doing his job. Didn't he realise? This was the most important day of her life. This was it. America!

They were far too early at the airport, even allowing for the fact that Danny had to get on the plane first, because of the wheelchair.

'We'll check the luggage in and have a coffee,' said Dad, who was acting as if he did this sort of thing all the time.

They all watched as 'Florida Fun' stickers were put on their borrowed suitcases.

'Next time we'll see those, we'll be in Orlando,' said Emma.

'You hope!' Dad grinned. 'As long as they go on the

same plane as us. Come on. We've got two hours yet!'

In the departure lounge they realised that they were starving. No-one had wanted an early breakfast. Mum went very generous and bought a pile of croissants and a jug of coffee.

'Hang on, Danny. Tablets.' She caught hold of his hands as he reached for a croissant.

'Mum, not here,' hissed Emma. 'People are looking.'

Mum just gave Danny his handful of tablets. 'Look, Emma, you know he has to have them. Every meal. Every snack. You don't want him took bad, do you?'

'Stop fussing!' Danny was cross. 'Just get on with it.' He wolfed down the flaky pastries, great crumbs littering his new outfit, a football shirt and shorts in the red and white of City's colours.

Emma went over to the huge plate glass windows to watch the planes. Danny came up to her. He could walk a little bit until he got too breathless. He stood next to her, thin and small, looking more like an eight than a ten year old. The football shorts made his white legs look more stick-insect like than ever, so that his new, white trainers plumped up on the end of them looked ridiculous, like a cartoon character. Holding his bony hand in her strong, firm one, Emma thought he would look a lot better when he had got a tan.

All around people were chatting, reading, having snacks and playing about with the contents of their hand luggage. Apart from one or two smiles it could have been a waiting room anywhere. Why wasn't everyone leaping about with excitement?

The pilot and crew marched solemnly past down a walkway and at last it was time to board. The Fishers went first, Danny triumphantly leading the procession in his chair. When he was safely stowed on board, next to a window, the rest of the holidaymakers surged onto the plane.

Emma sat with Dad by her window seat. This was it!

'Britannia welcomes you aboard' proclaimed the green writing on the small screen above their heads. People sorted themselves out, overhead locker doors were banged shut, seat belts checked by cheerful stewardesses, and a film started on safety procedures.

They were moving. Taxiing down the runway. Stop. Turn. Face the long ribbon of cold concrete. Emma felt scared and she wanted to hold Dad's hand, but was too old for that. Instead she crossed all her fingers and toes and took some deep breaths.

A powerful thrust surged through the Boeing 767 and they raced along the runway. And up, the ground falling away from them, like in a film. Higher and higher until they were thousands of feet in the air with only a few centimetres of metal and glass separating them from the sky.

'How long does it take, Dad?'

'About eight and a half hours. We refuel at Bangor, Maine, and then fly down the coast to Orlando.'

The coast! America's coast!

As Emma drank her Coke, complete with ice and lemon, she stared out of the window.

'We're just passing over Ireland,' came the voice known as 'This Is Your Captain Speaking'. 'Visibility is a little variable but there is a good view of the coastline below.'

Ireland's coast, thought Emma, and we've only been going a few minutes.

'We have headwinds of one hundred miles per hour

so this will keep our speed down below six hundred. Have a nice trip.'

Emma felt as if she was hardly moving and certainly not at hundreds of miles an hour. The sky was bluer than she would have thought possible and clouds like mounds of softly-whipped cream piped their way beneath them. Small clots had broken off and the whole scene reminded Emma of the way Mum iced a cake. One great white mass with bits splattered everywhere.

Through the gaps in the clouds, the sea shimmered like a sheet of steel, reflecting the fierce glare of the sun. What looked like tiny ripples from here but were in fact huge waves, hardly spoilt the greeny-blue depths. Here and there miniature islands poked their way inquisitively through the sparkling sea.

Lunch was fun. The Fishers all swapped bits out of their trays of pre-packed food. Emma ate three mini cheesecakes, while Dad finished off everyone's broccoli, and they all had refills of tea in their cute, navy blue, plastic cups.

'Like being inside a doll's house,' said Dad, angling his tall frame to retrieve dropped bits of packaging. 'Sue, I'll do Danny, give you a break.'

'Are you sure, Mark?' They swapped seats. Dad laid Danny over his knees and propped him up with a pile of pillows.

'You can't do it here!' said Emma.

Dad smiled. 'Three times a day, half an hour at a time, wherever he is,' he said, giving Danny his inhaler before working on his chest to clear his lungs. At the resultant coughing and spluttering people started to look. Emma went to queue for the loo. Mum was already patiently explaining to a couple of old ladies that children with cystic fibrosis, CF, had to do this . . . or else. Emma hated the pitying looks on their faces but Danny ignored them.

Wobbling about in the loo, Emma had a wash just to play about with the taps and soap dispenser. She looked good in her new T-shirt and matching shorts with beach umbrellas all over them. Fortunately her spots had cleared up after weeks of smothering her face with medicated skin cream. For once she felt good about herself.

Pressing the loo flush she jumped with shock. Horrendous gurgling threatened her. She was glad that she was not sitting on it, as she was sure some huge monster lurked inside, waiting to suck her, bottom first, down the hole and into outer space.

Time sped by and This Is Your Captain Speaking told them to prepare to land. All seats were pushed upright, the fold-down tables fastened securely and hand luggage stowed carefully away.

They were going towards the ground at four hundred and ninety miles per hour. The monitor ticked off the feet, twenty-seven thousand and falling by one thousand feet in twenty-six seconds. At this rate they would hit the ground in – let's see – five minutes? No, that could never be right.

Forgetting that she was supposed to be mature, Emma hung on to Mum's hand. Why aren't I falling forwards? Why hasn't my seat belt tightened? This is amazing. It's not even as bumpy as the number fifty-seven bus back home and I'm falling out of the sky.

'Here, Em, suck these, for your ears,' said Mum.

Sucking furiously, Emma could see the land rushing to meet her – straight roads, a muddy estuary, no skyscrapers or freeways, but clumps of forest and odd homesteads.

Ten thousand feet. Wing flaps up. Two hundred and seventy miles per hour. I'm falling. My ears! Everyone's gone quiet, all watching, waiting.

'You look like Dumbo,' laughed Mum, as Emma clasped two small, white pillows to her ears.

Two thousand feet. Rocking around. I want to get off, thought Emma. What's that weird, winding noise? We're going to hit the tops of the greeny-black fir trees. Where's the city? The airport?

One hundred and thirty miles per hour. Some sort of army base. Old bombers, like grounded whales with black backs and white bellies, straddled an overgrown runway.

Down! Emma started to breathe again. The maiden flight was over. Through the window she glimpsed weather-beaten concrete buildings and old hangars. No stars and stripes. This was not what America was supposed to look like!

'It's ten past twelve, Eastern Standard Time. We will be refuelling and should take off in thirty minutes. Please stay seated.'

Eastern Standard Time. It must be America then.

After refuelling, another meal and three more hours in the sky, nose glued to the window, it was time to land at Orlando.

'Look, Emma, Florida,' said Danny, calling from his seat. 'Can you see Mickey Mouse?'

'You nutter! Look at the lakes. Can you see Disneyworld?'

'It's a few miles away,' said Old Lady Number One who had talked to Mum non-stop since Bangor. She had been before and knew everything worth knowing.

'You'll want Interstate Four, off the end of International Drive . . .' She was off again.

Banking gently, the plane eased itself comfortably out of the sky. Everyone was talking at once and the music was blasting out, 'We're going to America!' It was not true. They were here!

Last off the plane, they trundled Danny into Orlando airport. It was huge. Armed security men directed them to passport control where they stood patiently in line before being allowed into the country.

To Emma's surprise they let Dad in. He looked nothing like his passport photo which did not show up the grey in his curly hair. It did not show the curls either as he had had the photo taken just after his last haircut! Dad only got his hair cut when he was on short time at the factory and looking for extra work. Emma could not understand why wanting an evening job trying to sell double glazing over the telephone meant Dad had to be scalped. Anyway he had only kept the job a few days and was now threatening to take up window cleaning when they got back home.

Emma pulled herself up with a start. Got back! They had only just got here. She would forget about Birmingham for the next two weeks.

'Now, the luggage,' said Dad, as they waited for their bags to appear miraculously on a conveyor belt.

'Mum, the loos flush on their own,' said Emma, grabbing her suitcase. 'Why isn't it hot? You said it would be hot.'

'Air-conditioning,' Danny informed her. 'They have it everywhere.' His near memorisation of the guide books was going to come in useful. 'They'll have it on the coach that takes us to the car-hire place.' He looked tired, but then he usually did. So did Dad and Mum, but it was a happy tiredness, not their usual worn-out, sad sort.

Luggage collected, they went to the coach meeting point. Huge glass doors opened automatically as they stepped outside.

It was like having a hot, wet blanket thrown over them. Even in the shade the heat was amazing. A straggly palm tree waved its fringed fronds in welcome.

Emma smiled and took the deepest breath ever. Her lungs filled with American air. Sweat started to form into tiny droplets and run down her back. This was it. Emma Fisher was in Florida. It was not a dream but a dream come true.

Chapter Three

In the sizzling heat of mid-afternoon the coach deposited them at the car hire office. Hundreds of tourists slowly melted in the sunshine as with great speed and efficiency, people were matched to their freshly washed cars.

'Have a nice day!' said a beaming face as Danny tipped her a few dollars. 'My, you have got a lot of luggage.' Expertly she packed spare bags round Danny and Emma in the back seat, at the same time as telling Dad how to drive and work the air-conditioning. On the dashboard a huge notice, in red letters, proclaimed, 'Drive on the right at all times!' just in case they forgot.

'Come on, Dad, I've had enough of this heat!' complained Emma.

'Enough! We've only just got here.'

'You know what I mean. Let's go.'

Slowly the Dodge Spirit joined the other cars on the road.

'Is this the freeway?' asked Danny.

'The what?' said Dad.

'Like our motorway.'

Mum, who was map-reading answered. 'No, it's an ordinary road. We've got to go a few miles to our apartment. Now let me concentrate.' She was baking hot in her usual T-shirt and jeans. Emma was looking forward to seeing her in shorts and sundresses. She could not really imagine what Mum would look like with her legs on show.

Through the window . . . well, the part not blocked by a suitcase . . . Emma drank in her first glimpses of Florida. They were crawling along a wide dual carriage-way as long cars glided past them. Dad was fiddling with the air conditioning. He had got it blasting out so much that Emma's arms were covered in goose pimples.

There was so much space and colour. A few buildings sprawled out, then an expanse of grass so green it looked as if it had been painted, then another motel or shop selling cut-price T-shirts, four for ten dollars. It was so spread out, nothing like the cramped, curving streets at home where every house was carefully separated from the road by a four foot high privet hedge. It was as if the Americans had thought, hey, we've got a lot of space so let's use it.

And the colours! A hotel in green and pink, another with huge turquoise fish on top of it and sea-blue waves painted up the sides! And there, *purple*, a motel in purple! And what about the signs? Perched on high poles, neon signs lured them to eat out, visit a show, buy souvenirs or drop in at McDonalds.

'I'm starving,' said Danny. 'Can we go to McDonalds?'

'You can't be,' said Mum. 'I know you have to eat a lot, but surely, you're not hungry yet.'

'Am.' He put on his irresistible cheeky grin that lit up his entire face.

'Well, let's find the apartment first. Mark, I think we should have turned off, back at the last set of lights.'

'Why didn't you say? I can't U-turn here. It's all right for you lot, gawping out of the windows, but this driving is no picnic.' He drove on while Mum got him more and more confused.

Eventually they found their apartment block, purely by luck, as according to Mum they were not even in the right part of town.

It was beautiful. There was a lake with a fountain pluming up into the darkening sky. At one end lay a swimming pool surrounded by a paved area and all around the lake were apartments.

There were three on top of each other, painted in salmon pink, that made them look as if they had been hugged by the warm sun.

'Ah, Mr and Mrs Fisher, and this must be Danny,' said the man on reception, ignoring Emma. 'I've put you in 101, that's block one, ground floor. It's right by the pool. Thought that would be easier.'

'Thanks.'

'No problem. Did you have a good flight? We sure hope you enjoy your stay. Any queries, Stan's your man.'

Emma grabbed the key and ran off.

'Em, give us a hand with . . .' but she had gone.

Emma thought that the apartment was ace. The only drawback was that she would have to share a bedroom with Danny, and if he started coughing in the night, she would never sleep. But what a bedroom! It was immense, the two beds metres apart, with its own bathroom, a walk-in wardrobe where her clothes would look lost, its own television, furniture in pale wood, and a couple of strange-looking paintings hanging on the wall. The bedspreads and carpet were matching peach, and a Venetian blind covered the window.

Emma raised it. The room overlooked the fountain which whooshed into the sky.

'Emma! Come and help!' Dad staggered in like an overladen camel. 'Mum's got to do Danny's physio, so you can help unload the car.'

This was the trouble, thought Emma. When anything needed doing it was always her. At home it did not matter, she was used to it. But here! There were so many more exciting things to do than heave suitcases around.

'We'll unpack later. I'm nipping out for some supplies and burgers. Coming?'

'Sure thing, man,' said Emma in an appalling imitation of an American accent.

'Stan's your man' told them where the supermarket was. 'Just a block away' took them ten minutes to drive. Although it was now dark, all the shops were open and Emma had a great time choosing food.

'Mum said just a few basics,' protested Dad, as Emma put six huge bottles of Coke in the shopping trolley. 'We'll eat out some of the time. She just wants us to get enough to tide us over.'

'I can't find baked beans,' said Emma, 'and are these things sausages?'

'Well, don't expect it to be like the supermarkets at home,' said Dad. 'These cereals are expensive. We'll have pancakes.'

'Pancakes! For breakfast!'

'You know what they say, "when in Rome do as the Romans do".'

'But this is Orlando, Dad.'

'Same difference!'

They were both impressed by the service at the cash desk. An older man packed all their stuff into thick, brown bags that were printed with hurricane evacuation procedures. The cashier helped Dad sort out his one dollar bills from the tens and twenties.

'They're all the same colour,' Dad complained.

'Sure,' smiled the cashier. 'You from England?'

'Yes, just. How did you know?'

She laughed. 'Oh, the accent . . . it's so cute. And that!' she pointed to Dad's T-shirt – England Football. 'Wasn't hard to guess. Have a nice day!'

'Dad,' said Emma in the car, after they had stopped off for burgers, 'do they always say that nice day stuff, even at night?'

Dad laughed. 'We'll see. Anyway she thought I was cute.'

'Cute! Your accent, not you!'

Once the burgers were demolished, Mum said it was time for bed. Emma insisted that she was not tired, which was strangely true, despite the hours she had been awake and the time difference. She persuaded her parents to let her go into the pool.

'I'll come down in a bit,' called Dad. 'Be careful and don't pester anyone.'

In her new swimming costume Emma walked slowly to the floodlit pool. Irene Watkins' Tenerife beach towel was casually thrown over one shoulder. She felt like a film star as she strolled along with her head held high. Pity she hadn't, well, developed they called it, a bit more, like Justine and the others. It would make her look older. She would casually drape her towel over a chair and dive gracefully into the pool while everyone gasped in amazement at her skill and agility.

The film star came to earth with a shriek.

'Aagh! What is it?' Something had slithered over her bare foot. A lizard still active in the warm night! At that moment a moth, that Emma swore later was the size of a bat, brushed past her face, causing her to scream again.

'You okay?' a head bobbing in the pool called to her. 'Come on in.'

'I'm fine. It's, well, these things.'

'Get them everywhere. What you expect in a sub-tropical climate?'

Flipping know-all, thought Emma, carefully getting into the silky warm water.

'You here on holiday? You're very white,' said the head. 'I'm Josh.'

'Yes, I'm Emma. We're from England.' Emma did not want to talk. She wanted to lie there in the water and think. It was amazing. Back home it was one o'clock in the morning and yet here she was, lying in an outdoor pool, warm and relaxed. Above her a velvety-black sky stretched endlessly. It was so dark and soft-looking, she wanted to reach out and stroke it. Around her people were splashing and calling to one another, yet Emma felt as if she were the only person in the world.

Flat on her back she let the water fill her ears, until all the sounds distorted into a mumbled thump bump. I'm me, she thought. I'm me, in a pool, in sub-tropical Florida. I'll always be me. I'll never be anyone else. I can't be Mum or Dad or Danny or anyone. All of a sudden she felt very small, floating there under the endless sky.

I want to remember this for ever, she thought, shutting her eyes. She re-ran the day's events in her mind, deliberately stopping at different points. It's like taking photos, she thought, I can take them in my mind and they can stay with me for ever.

She had got to the part where the cashier called Dad cute, when a surge of water overturned her and left her spluttering.

'It's only me,' said Josh, long, black hair sticking to his face and covering one eye. 'Didn't want you to go to sleep. I'm here with Mum and Leroy.'

'Leroy?' Emma asked, before she could stop herself. 'Who's that?'

'That's Mum's boyfriend, well, man. He's gross. Dad cleared out ages ago and I reckon Leroy thinks he can be my new dad. He's a prize idiot. I'm from Chicago. Know where that is? Up north.' Josh's teeth gleamed oddly in the glare of the lights. He had a silvery brace riveted to them and in the dancing light looked like a friendly sea monster, telling her his life story. 'Let's race round the pool. Go!'

Emma chased after him, colliding with other swimmers until, breathless, they stopped for a rest. Dad appeared and watched, pleased to see Emma making a new friend.

'Emma, time to go!' She peeled herself out of the pool, followed by Josh.

'Okay, Dad.' She would not protest in front of Josh. 'This is Josh, from Chicago.'

'Ah, a gangster!'

'Pardon, sir?'

'Sir! Well any friend of yours who calls me sir can't be bad. Come along, Emma. Another full day tomorrow. Night, Josh.'

Chapter Four

'Emma! Get up! It's nearly time to go.' Mum was shaking her bed. 'The meeting is in less than an hour, and we've got to find it.'

Stretching, Emma threw off the thin blanket and staggered out of bed. Luxurious, thick, soft carpet tufted up between her toes and the first thing she was aware of was the whirring sound of the air conditioning. Eight o'clock! She had slept for hours and where was Danny?

'He's in the pool with Dad,' said Mum, catching her glance. 'It'll give him the chance to get used to it, while it's nearly empty.'

'Of water?' joked Emma. She was pleased to see that Mum was wearing a sundress. Emma thought how nice she looked. That blue colour really suited her and somehow made her eyes look bigger and greener than usual.

'You know what I mean. I've got a stack of pancakes in the microwave and we'll try them with maple syrup.'

They were scrumptious, if you ignored the still-frozen bits in the middle. Danny ate loads. It was odd the way he ate twice as much as her, thought Emma, yet was so thin. She knew his digestive system did not work properly, which was why he had to have lots of enzyme tablets with each meal. However, there must be some advantages of eating everything he could and never getting fat. She would have to watch it, she thought. This food was ace and if she was not careful she would be developing all right, but in all the wrong places!

'Mum, do I need the wheelchair? I can walk to the car and we've only got to sit at the other end at the welcome meeting,' Danny pleaded, his chest already heaving with the effort of breathing.

'Look, Danny, if you don't use the chair now, you'll be too shattered to do anything later, so don't make a fuss, there's a a good lad.' Mum was patient, but firm.

'Okay,' he grinned, showing his super-white teeth. 'On one condition. You get an English newspaper. I've got to read how City got on.'

'You win,' said Mum. Danny usually did. 'Let's go.'

The welcome meeting was in a place all done up like a Wild West fort. Even Mum found it easily, which was not surprising seeing that wigwams, a totem pole and life-sized models of Indians on horseback stretched along the roadside in front of it.

'Didn't think they had Indians in Florida,' said Dad.

'Shush!' Mum was treating him like a child. 'Let's look around the courtyard before we go into the fort.'

After exhausting the displays and shops, they were herded into the fort. It had been made to look old, with dark wood everywhere and walls covered with Indian headdresses, old flags, bits of saddlery and ancient pots and pans. It was dark after the glare outside and more than one person stumbled over the wheelchair.

Emma looked around. There were lots of people from their flight, but how different they looked. Old Lady Number One had changed from being like anyone's grandma and was now wearing white shorts, a pink, sleeveless T-shirt, strappy sandals and a huge sunhat, with a pink, floaty scarf tied to it. She seemed to have gone brown overnight. When Emma pointed that out, Mum said it was probably out of a bottle.

'Welcome everyone,' said their smiling hostess, appropriately dressed as a cowgirl complete with white stetson hat. 'We're going to fill you in on all the attractions, give you the opportunity to buy tickets at discount prices, and let you into a few secrets on the American way of life. Do help yourselves to coffee or orange juice.'

Emma listened to the wonders of Disneyworld, which were spread out over a number of sites, Sea World, the Studios, Wet 'n' Wild . . . The list went on.

'And so we suggest you use the day planner, on the table, to work out what you want to do and when. Then any of the hosts or hostesses will sell you your tickets.'

Danny had already filled in his planner. A major visit every day.

'Grief, Danny! Are you trying to kill us off?' protested Dad. 'We'll never keep up that pace. Your mum's not as young as she used to be.'

Mum smiled. 'Cheeky! And I'm a year younger than you, Mark.'

'Anyway, we'll have one busy day, then a quieter one. And we've got to make sure that the money lasts out.' Dad was waving it around as though it were out of a Monopoly game.

A new thought struck Emma. Mum and Dad often joked with each other when Danny was there. She realised they were doing it to be nice to him. It was not that they could not keep up the pace. It was Danny, and they did not want him to feel bad about it. Trouble was, Emma had to slow down too. For the first time in her life she asked herself what she felt about that. At home it did not matter. But here? Everything was different and she wanted to go everywhere, do everything.

And then it happened. Danny had been laughing at some joke or other when he started to cough. When he coughed he certainly knew how to do it. Wheezing, gulping, spluttering. His face starting to turn an odd shade of pale blue.

'Has his drink gone down the wrong way?' asked the young, trendy man sitting next to them.

'Pat his back,' said his girlfriend. 'He'll choke.'

'It's okay,' replied Dad. 'It doesn't happen too much in public. He'll be fine soon. He knows what to do.'

It did not look as if he did. Danny's undersized body topped by the tuft of gelled hair was racked with spasms. People were staring, or pretending not to look, which was just as bad. Couldn't they see how insensitive they were being?

'It shouldn't be allowed,' the high pitched, well-educated voice of a woman nearby pierced its way like an arrow through the general hubbub of noise. 'Spoils the holiday for the children, seeing him like that.'

At that moment Danny coughed up his usual gunge into the pot Mum always had with her. He took some deep breaths and slowly returned to normal. Mum ruffled his hair, ruining the gelled tuft.

'Don't take any notice, Danny,' she whispered.

'Should be with a special party for the disabled,' the high voice whined on.

Emma felt her cheeks burning. Without thinking she leapt to her feet and stormed over to the woman.

'What do you know?' she yelled, fists clenched and

unbidden tears springing into her eyes. 'You know nothing! He's my brother. He's got CF. He's been in hospital loads of times. Don't you dare say things about him. He can come on holiday like anyone else. You leave him alone, you . . . you . . . great . . .' Words failed her, words that she dared repeat.

'Well, really!' High Voice stood up, bursting out of her sundress and clanking with gold jewellery. 'What on earth . . . ?'

'I'm sorry, madam,' said Dad, intervening. 'Emma did not mean it.'

'Did,' hissed his daughter.

'I hope we have not distressed you, but coughing fits are a way of life for us.' Dad pulled Emma away. 'Go outside and calm down,' he told her.

'But Dad . . .'

'Go!'

Emma sulked off. Mum was explaining all about cystic fibrosis to the young, trendy couple. They were nice. Not like that old hag in there, thought Emma. What right had she got to talk about Danny like that, the stupid old bat? Emma felt like throttling her. How dare anyone treat her brother that way! All Emma's protective instincts surged up. She wanted to pull the woman's hair out, strand by strand. Hope she drops dead, she thought.

She paced up and down the courtyard waiting for the others. Slowly she calmed down in the heat. If Dad told her off she would go mad.

Dad joined her. 'Emma,' he said, looking her straight in the eye. 'It's okay. That woman did not know what she was saying. She just wasn't used to someone like Danny.'

'Well, she should have been.'

'Em, at home everyone knows us. They are used to us, but here it's different. Whether we like it or not, people are prejudiced and we have to put up with it.'

'It's not fair!'

'I know, but it's a fact. How about the pool again, hey?'

They spent the rest of the day lazing in and around the pool. At least in the water Danny looked no different from anyone else. His legs were very weak so Dad or Mum had to be with him or watch him as he lay floating, a long white streak, on his red air bed.

'Hey, where you all been?' Josh dived into the pool. 'Looked for you this morning.'

'Oh, nowhere.' Emma wanted to forget today's fiasco. 'This is my brother Danny. He's ten.'

'Makes me a year older. Come on, Danny, let's have a diving competition.'

'He can't. He's ill.'

Josh whistled. 'Tough! I know what, like us to push you around on the air bed, Danny?'

'Great!' Lying on his stomach on the air bed Danny was jet-propelled through the water, shrieking with laughter.

'Drinks, Josh,' called a golden body, gleaming with sun tan oil. 'Bring your friends.'

'It's my mum. Come on.'

Mrs Everett, Josh's mum, had already made friends with Sue Fisher.

'Hi! I'm Angie, now let's see who is who.' She organised them expertly and they chatted as they worked their way through two bottles of Coke. Mrs Everett's eyes opened wide as Danny took a couple of tablets before his drink, but at least she said nothing.

She was the smartest woman Emma had ever seen in real life. Up until now she had thought people like Josh's mum only existed in glossy magazines. Everything about her was glamorous from the towelling wrap slung casually round her shoulders to the elegant way she sat up and carefully crossed her legs.

She looked about twenty, her eyes hidden behind huge black sunglasses but she must have been a lot older to be Josh's mum.

I can't imagine her rushing round the supermarket or doing piles of ironing, thought Emma, grinning at the picture that she had conjured up in her mind. I wish I looked like she does.

Emma tried to sit down gracefully on the patio, gently folding her legs beneath her. The effect was spoiled when her knees made a funny cracking noise and she landed on her backside with a thump that sent shudders through her body. Never mind, she would watch how Angie did it and by the time she went back to school she would be the envy of all her friends.

A huge giant of a man came to the poolside. His faded blue jeans were tucked into real leather, cowboy boots and his well-rounded, bare chest sprouted a mat of grey hairs. Under his baseball cap his tanned face was cracked into deep lines and he was chewing gum. He looked ancient, at least fifty, thought Emma.

'Hi, honey. How's Leroy's little angel?' Josh squirmed with embarrassment as Leroy cupped his mum's golden hand, with its perfectly manicured fingernails, in his great hairy one. Emma was fascinated. Leroy and Angie could provide hours of fun.

'Better for seeing you, honey bun,' simpered Angie.

'Now, meet Sue, Mark, Emma and Danny. All the way from Birmingham, England, *not* Alabama.' She giggled like a child.

Josh dived into the pool and Emma followed him.

'See what I mean! Gross! The best thing about those two is that they leave me well alone.'

'They're fun,' said Emma.

'Fun! You Brits are crazy. Imagine living with that, all the time.'

Emma was quiet. Surely that must be better than living all the time with a little brother whom she loved so much, yet who kept on being so ill. Josh did not know how lucky he was.

Chapter Five

The Magic Kingdom opened at nine o'clock and the Fishers were determined to be there early. After driving slowly and following the signs, they reached the parking lot. Concrete stretched as far as they could see, broken only by clumps of trees.

'We'll leave the car here in the shade,' said Dad, already sweating in the heat. He was wearing blue and white shorts and matching T-shirt, topped by his 'Captain Florida' baseball hat which stuck up above his thick, dark, curly hair. Expertly, he flipped Danny into his fold-up wheelchair. They got on the tram and were driven to the ticket centre where they joined the queues already formed.

'I can't even see it,' said Emma. 'Where's the castle, the rides?'

'It says here,' said Mum, waving her guide, 'that we've got to get a ferry or monorail next.'

'Monorail!' chorused Danny and Emma, and within minutes they were gliding speedily along over lakes and past hotels.

'It's there!' Cinderella's Castle poked up through the trees and buildings, gleaming white in the sunshine, as if it had just come straight out of the washing machine.

'Can we go there first?'

'No, Space Mountain,' said Danny.

'Go on, Mum, then Frontierland,' pleaded Emma.

'I want to go to Tomorrowland, on Space Mountain,' insisted Danny.

Mum sighed. 'All right, you two. Plenty of time for everything. What's it suggest, Mark, in the disabled guests' guidebook?'

'Start at Tomorrowland,' said Dad, trundling the wheelchair at speed through people wandering along Main Street.

Disabled guests! thought Emma. What a cheek! Nothing disabled about her. She could do what she wanted to, like everyone else.

She looked at people around her. Everyone eager, suppressed excitement showing in the bouncy way they walked. People smiling, wearing brightly-coloured clothes, animated faces, laughing and joking. It was so different to the drab, grey High Street back home where worried, grey shoppers shuffled along, weighed down by bags of food, or trailed tired toddlers. This was a different world.

'Look, Dad.' Danny pointed to a horse-drawn tram that rolled past him.

'I'm going in here,' called Emma, heading towards a shop.

'Em, wait! We've all got to stay together.'

'Oh, *Dad*.'

'Yes. This place is huge. Just slow down. Look, we'll buy one of those silvery-black Mickey Mouse balloons and tie it to the chair, then we can see where it is and stay together.'

'But Dad, I'm twelve!'

'Yes, and this is a foreign country. Stay put.'

Foreign country, my foot! thought Emma. Slow down! How could she? There was so much to go on and they had done nothing yet. Somehow she kept her legs from running away.

At last they got to Space Mountain – 'A high speed, turbulent, roller coaster ride through space!'

'I don't know,' said Mum. 'I mean, it might be a bit much for Danny. It says here you've got to climb and walk in case of an evacuation situation. I don't like the sound of that.'

'He'll be okay,' said Dad.

Emma sighed. They were at it again. If they discussed whether Danny could go on things at every ride, they would do nothing!

Dad won the argument, they joined the queue, the line-up as the Americans called it, and eventually were strapped into their rockets.

It was brilliant! Shooting and twisting through the dark while stars and planets whizzed past. Emma clung on tightly as her body contorted through the ride, whirling first this way and that. Turbulent! It was terrifying!

'You okay, Sue?' asked Dad when they had got off. Mum had gone green in the face and was shivering in spite of the heat.

'Don't you ever, ever take me on one of those again!'

'It was ace, Mum!' said Danny. 'Did you see Saturn and Mars?'

'I didn't see much at all. I kept my eyes shut. It was awful!' moaned Mum, but she did not get much sympathy as they were already off to the next attraction. She trailed behind them, still looking sick. Her brown straight hair was already sticking to her head in the sweaty heat so she tied it back in a short ponytail which made her look years younger.

One ride merged into another. Danny and Dad would wait at the special disabled entrance until Mum and Emma had got to the front of their slow-moving line-up. Then Danny would either be wheeled to a viewing area to watch a show, or the ride would stop so he could slowly climb aboard.

All the time the sun shone, and disembodied voices urged them to stay in line, move to the end of the row and have a nice day.

'Lunch,' said Dad, as they emerged from a Disney character song and dance show.

'Lunch! Can't be. We've only done this bit, and there's loads more to do,' protested Emma.

'Why do you think it is open till midnight? Now,' Dad read the guide, 'are we for healthy eating with frozen yoghurt and fruit juices, or pizza?'

'Pizza!'

As they ate huge, bubbling wedges of pizza in the outdoor café, a pianist, dressed like Pluto, played tunes only Dad knew. Cheeky, bluey-black birds darted and stole crumbs, despite notices telling people not to feed them. Emma let her eyes drink in the view. Fountains sparkled in the fresh air and through them she could see the fairy tale castle dominating the scene.

They took the Skyway, a sort of cable car, to Fantasyland, where, as the guidebook told them, storybook dreams come true.

'I'm too old for all of this,' said Emma, itching to get to another area of the park. 'Flying Dumbos and twirling teacups are not for me.'

Fortunately, no-one took any notice and Emma found

herself enjoying Captain Nemo on the Nautilus going twenty thousand leagues under the sea, before riding the galloping horses on the golden carousel. It was as if everyone had become the same age, children, teenagers, parents, old people, all as one, rushing around, lining up and enjoying the rides – all except the toddlers wasting the experience by falling fast asleep in their buggies. Emma felt about six years old, but it did not matter. Everybody did.

'Time for the parade. Got to get Danny into position.' Dad squeezed them all into the special viewing area. At three o'clock music blasted out and the parade began. Emma had expected a few floats and some fancy dress but not this! What a sight!

The band, in patriotic red, white and blue, feathers dancing on their hats, marched past, followed by dancers, all keeping in step. How could they wear costumes and dance in this heat and all the time keep on smiling?

'Look at the horses,' pointed out Danny, as they clopped past, their coats shiny and soft like conkers newly prised out of their shells. 'Donald Duck's on that one.'

'Wonder what would happen if his head fell off?' said Emma.

A gigantic float lumbered by, made to look like a mountain, then one like a gold mine. Girls on roller skates, with impossibly long hair, twirled and danced. Lads on skateboards shot down the next float, doing jumps and turns. Even Tigger, his stiffened tail never deviating from its S shape, zoomed past on his skateboard.

'Wish I could do that,' said Danny, wistfully. Emma just smiled at him. If only Danny could run around like most children. Emma could not understand why he never complained or went on about his CF. It was almost as if he pretended it was not real. Yet Emma knew that deep down inside, her brother longed to be able to do what his friends could.

Danny's skateboard had not come out of the garden shed for a very long time. He would never twirl and pirouette like this. Never. Emma suddenly felt very sad but forced herself to escape back into the magic that was going on all around her.

After the grotesque, wicked Queen from Alice in Wonderland and her float had gone, there came the grand finale. On what looked like a life-sized paddle-steamer, an ever-smiling Mickey Mouse in a white, satin suit studded with large silver sequins waved at everyone, while his companion Minnie Mouse shouted squeaky greetings to the cheering crowd.

'What do you think, Danny?' said Mum, bending down to be on his level.

'This,' he said slowly, 'is the happiest day of my life.'

His gelled tuft of hair had collapsed in the heat, his mouth was smeared with pizza stains and he had spilt Coke down his new T-shirt. Hands clasped together, he leant forward in the wheelchair and repeated, 'The happiest day of my life.'

They had to leave after the parade. Emma kicked up a fuss. Dad got hold of her.

'We need a rest. We'll come back after tea. And there's Danny's physio.'

'But I could stay and meet you later. I'll be good.'

'No way. Now, no fuss.' Dad's voice took on a pleading quality. 'He's worn out.'

'In a wheelchair! Don't be daft. He hasn't walked miles like me.' Emma sulked into silence. Go back and leave this magical world three-quarters untouched! It isn't fair, she thought. I'll never get the chance again. It's all Danny's fault. Why can't he be normal? Why can't he just keep going, like anyone else? She glanced at him, eyes half-closed, as Dad helped him into the car and sent her a warning glance.

'Can't me and Mum stay? You do his physio?'

'Emma, it's hot, well over ninety degrees, we're tired, we're having a rest. That's it. Understood?'

Emma grunted in reply. They could rest but she would go off to the pool. Find someone proper to play with. Someone like Josh.

While the others saw to Danny and rested, Emma lazed in the cool of the pool. The water relaxed her as the sun slowly grilled her exposed skin, covered in cream, and she started to turn golden brown.

After a tea of sandwiches and fruit they drove back to the Magic Kingdom. Actually, now it was darker, it was not so hot, so they could all keep going longer, only stopping a few times for drinks from the water fountains dotted around.

As they left the park at midnight, Emma decided that after all it was a good idea to have a rest day. Her ears buzzed with all the different music mixed up inside them, like paints on an artist's palette. Images from countless films and shows flashed in front of her eyes, and her stomach did not know whether she had just come off a gentle Caribbean cruise or was recovering from another rollercoaster.

The smell of hot pretzels and salty popcorn mingled in the warm night air and Emma breathed it in deeply. She wanted to keep all the sounds, smells, sights and sensations of today wrapped deep inside her forever. The Magic Kingdom was truly magic!

Chapter Six

'Hi there, Emma. Going for a dip?'

'Hello, Mrs Everett. Is Josh about?'

'He's in the jacuzzi. And Emma, call me Angie. Mrs Everett makes me sound so ancient!'

'Okay, Angie!' Emma could not resist staring at the glamorous woman. Long golden legs fitted into a perfect body wearing a bikini like a second skin. Her sunglasses were perched on top of her head with tiny strands of blond hair curling over them. It must have taken ages to get it like that. The smell of warm coconut sun tan oil wafted around her, not like this smelly stuff Mum had plastered on Emma.

The jacuzzi was a bubbling hot tub, like a round bath next to the pool and Emma joined Josh, only their heads showing above the frothing steam.

'Where are you going today?' asked Josh, squinting at her through long, dark eyelashes, as the sun shone full on his deeply-tanned face.

'Nowhere! Would you believe it, here we are thousands of miles from home and we're going nowhere. I ask you!'

'Ask me what?' Josh was puzzled.

'Nothing. It's just a saying. Anyway, what are you

doing?'

'Oh, this and that. Pool, fitness room, might play tennis. Mum,' he said, glancing at her reclining form, 'is topping up her tan, and the Bear has gone shopping.'

'The Bear?'

'Leroy. You must have seen his hairy chest. I reckon he shampoos it. What Mum sees in him, I don't know. Let's have a swim. Do you think we can use Danny's air bed?'

'Sure?'

The two of them invented a game. One stood on the side of the pool while the other stayed in the water holding the air bed steady. The idea was to leap from the side, land front downwards on the air bed and see how far the force of the landing could propel them across the pool.

'Be careful!' called Angie, half-heartedly. They were. Not that it made any difference to the final outcome. Emma took a mighty leap and landed splat in the middle of the air bed. There was a tearing noise, a rush of air, and Emma and bed sank into the pool.

'Emma! What on earth?' Trust Mum to turn up just then. 'You know that's Danny's. I sometimes wonder whether you've got any brains at all. Now, what are we going to do?'

Mum sounded back to normal, just like at home, nagging on. Emma would never hear the end of this!

'Hi, Sue.' Angie uncurled herself gracefully like a cat waking from a dreamless sleep. 'Don't worry. Leroy will go fetch another one.'

Mum stopped. She had not seen Angie and, fortunately for Emma, the sight of her calmed her down. She took a deep breath. 'I'm sure we can get another. It's

Danny, you see. He, well, he can't get around like the others, but he loves being in the pool.'

'With that cough? I'm not being nosy but I couldn't help hearing him last night. Won't it make it worse?'

'No. Anyway, it's not catching. It just makes him very tired and he can't do all the things he wants to. He's pretty ill.' Mum stated in a matter of fact way.

The two women chatted while Danny joined his sister and Josh in the pool. Dad was exploring the area on foot, though what he expected to find other than hotels and apartments was a mystery.

'He's very thin,' commented Angie, as Danny floated on his back with Emma standing guard next to him. 'He sure doesn't look ten.'

'Talking of thin,' said Mum, wanting to change the subject, 'we thought we'd try one of those "All you can eat for six dollars" places later on. Would you like to join us?'

Angie smiled and patted her firm flat stomach. 'Better not. Diet you know. But I'm sure Josh would like to join you. After all, he'd be company for Emma, and from what you've been telling me she's like an only child too.'

Her voice carried clearly across the pool, her words burning their way into the children's minds.

'You're not an only child, are you Emma?' said Danny, draping his arms around her neck. 'Are you?'

'Course not.' She tickled her brother. 'Fat chance I've got of being an only child with you around.'

'Well, why did she say it?' asked Danny, who had made an instant decision to hate Angie.

Josh looked embarrassed and to cover his confusion, he dived deep underwater and swam to the far end, leaving Emma to answer Danny's question. Emma did not know what to say. She was not used to people making negative remarks about her brother. Up until now everyone, including herself, had treated him as special and precious.

'I don't know. Perhaps she never thought. Look, don't let it get to you. You like Josh, don't you?'

'He's fun. I suppose it's not his fault his mum's a right idiot.' The cloud disappeared from Danny's face, but a small cloud started to creep, unasked and unwanted, into Emma's brain.

Just think, said the cloud, what it would be like to have a normal brother, or to be an only child. You wouldn't have to hang around here all day. You could be in Disneyworld. You could do what you wanted. So could Mum and Dad. There would be no physio three times a day, no coughing fits, and hospitals and Mum crying. You'd be free!

'Go away!' she said out loud. 'Stop it.' She submerged herself in the water to wash the creeping cloud away. What was happening? She had never had these thoughts before. Why now? She did not like them and was scared where they would lead. Danny was her brother, she loved him, for goodness sake, so why had these hateful thoughts come?

Emma dived under her brother. 'Do you want a rest, a sunbathe now? I'll play with you. I'll even ask you your football quiz questions,' she suggested, the ultimate sacrifice to make up for her thoughts.

'Great! Will you fetch them from the apartment? Here, heave me out of the water.'

Emma found the quiz, oblivious of the pools of water soaking into the carpet, and armed with a bottle of

Coke, a packet of biscuits and some bananas returned to the poolside. Danny was on a sunlounger as far away as possible from Mum and Angie.

'I'm not sitting near her,' he stated. 'Now ask the questions.'

Danny's encyclopaedic knowledge always amazed Emma. How anyone could remember who won the F. A. Cup in 1954, which team had been the longest in Division One, the names of the 1966 England World Cup team and what led to the penalty decision in some obscure game in September 1986 was beyond her. Even more strange was the fact that anyone would want to know such useless rubbish. It was so excruciatingly boring!

Josh joined in but knew even less about British football than Emma, which was saying something. Emma left them, with Danny explaining the rules by drawing all over the holiday brochure, and Josh arguing that American football was a far better game. So much for Josh being *her* friend.

'Food time.' Dad strolled to the poolside. 'Here, cheeky, got you this.' He threw Danny a two day old English newspaper. 'Cost me four dollars, and City lost. My, it's hot. I'll have a quick dip and then we'll be off.'

'Dad, can Josh come?' asked Emma.

Dad looked at Angie who nodded. 'Course.'

'And Dad, promise me one thing.'

'What Emma?'

'You won't wear socks with your sandals. You look daft.'

Dad glanced down past his 'Florida Fun' T-shirt in fluorescent pink and green, his black and white bermuda shorts, to the offensive socks. Obviously bright clothes were fine but white sports socks were definitely out.

The Dodge Spirit found the restaurant. They bought a cold drink and paid their six dollars each.

'You folks done this before? No? Well, you help yourselves to whatever you want, as much as you want, and your waiter will refill your glasses whenever you want. Have a nice day!'

A huge selection of food spread itself temptingly before them.

'Don't go mad,' said Mum, slipping Danny his handful of tablets. 'Control yourselves.' She was wasting her breath. It was three in the afternoon and they had not eaten since the poolside biscuits.

Emma had soup for starters, then spaghetti bolognese for another starter followed by spare ribs, three trips to the salad bar and then a rest while she waited for room to stuff down her dessert.

'These are ace,' said Danny, spearing round balls of something onto his fork. 'What are they?'

'Crab balls,' said Josh, who was enjoying telling them about all that was going on.

'Ugh!' Danny spluttered. 'I hate crab.' And he spat it out while Emma pretended not to be with him. Now everybody would be looking at the disgusting little toad. The thought cloud started to creep back into her mind. He was revolting!

Two and a half puddings and about a litre of Coke later, they returned to the pool. In the car Danny and Josh had a burping competition and Emma joined in, protesting that it was the Coke that make her do it. Dad told them off, but his remarks were spoilt by the huge burp he let out in mid-sentence.

'No more Coke for you lot, if this continues. Now,

no pool for at least an hour. I'm going for a lie down. Behave yourselves.' Mum stalked off to sleep off her dinner.

'Hi, I'm Darlene and this is Cindy. We're ten and a half.'

Emma blinked. She was nearly asleep on her lounger.

'We're from Colorado.' They spoke in unison.

'And we're half-Spanish.'

'That's the half that gives us our tan.'

Emma sat up. Two identical, brown faces with long straggly dark hair wrapped round them, like battered seaweed, stared at her.

'We're twins,' said one of them, unnecessarily, 'on vacation. Grandma's having a lie down and Grandad's watching baseball on TV.'

'Oh,' said Emma, unsure what to do with this information.

'You know what?' said one of them, 'Grandma says he is losing his brain.'

'It's falling out of his head,' said Number Two.

'He forgot to put his teeth in this morning.'

'And he didn't change his underpants. Does your dad?'

Emma nodded, surprised at the way the conversation was going.

'And,' said Number One, – or was it Two? – 'he went to the shop for bread and came back with a lemon tart.'

'And the other day he forgot where he parked the car.'

'No, that was Grandma, silly.'

'Anyway, he nearly threw up on the roller coaster and Grandma said he was too old to have his photo taken with Mickey Mouse.'

'It was Minnie! She said she didn't like the gleam in his eye.'

'Still took his photo though. That your mum?'

'No, it's Josh's,' said Emma. 'Where's yours?'

'Oh,' giggled Number Two. 'She's worn out. Grandma told Dad they'd bring us on vacation before she had a nervous breakdown! Isn't it funny?'

'Dad said he'd stay at home. He's painting the house. He wouldn't let us help. He's real mean. Do you know he can wiggle his ears? Come in the pool with us. Go on.'

Emma obliged, smiling. No wonder their mum was cracking up. They never stopped!

'Which of you is which?' she asked.

'I'm Darlene. You can tell because I've got more freckles on my arms than her. Look.'

Emma laughed and from then on could never tell them apart. Joined later by Josh, the five of them played in the pool until well after the sky had darkened and the moths had begun their nocturnal activities.

Chapter Seven

Next morning they set off early. Josh was joining them on a visit to the Epcot Centre, another part of Disney-world, while his mum and Leroy went shopping again.

'Another SSS,' said Josh. 'I'm sure glad you folks have gotten me along.'

'SSS?' queried Emma.

'Severe Shopping Session. Man, is it boring! Look, we're here.'

The huge, futuristic globe of Spaceship Earth, one hundred and eighty feet high, glinted silver in the morning light. It dwarfed the tall palm trees and the people lining up to get into Epcot looked like ants.

'Gee! Some geosphere!' whistled Josh. Emma did not know what he meant but nodded anyway. 'What a welcome to Futureworld!'

Epcot was ideally laid out for wheelchair guests and Danny could visit all the attractions. After watching a film where they felt they were inside a twelve year old boy's head, they rode a simulator which took them tearing through a human body. It really seemed as if they were shooting along arteries and down intestines.

'Brill,' said Danny. 'I'm going on one of these.' He pointed to a display of hands-on exhibits where computers could tell you anything about yourself.'

'Must we, Mum?' protested Emma. 'I want to go to the Living Seas?'

'I'll tell you what,' said Mum, 'if you promise to be at this restaurant at twelve-thirty, you and Josh can go off together. Don't mess about. Stay together and behave!' She turned to Mark. 'That way Danny can enjoy the computers in peace without those two nagging him every two seconds to hurry up.'

Like birds released from a cage, Josh and Emma flew off, their blond and dark heads bouncing through the gradually thickening crowd. They could run from one attraction to another and see much more than if they had to go at Danny's pace.

The Living Seas was fantastic. Sharks, dolphins and manatees swam in the world's largest man-made salt-water tank. Emma and Josh walked through the tank in glass-walled and roofed corridors.

'Look! A shark.' Emma pointed to the huge, pale belly drifting above her head, its horrific mouth split in an insane grin showing rows of flesh-tearing teeth. It was only a metre away from her. 'I hope this glass is strong!'

Oversized fish silently glided past. According to Josh they were all either guppas or baracuddas. If so, they came in lots of shapes and sizes. Emma could have watched them for hours but Josh was eager to be off.

'If we hurry,' he said, tugging at her arm and leaving white fingermarks on her sunburnt skin, 'we'll just make the next showing of Captain EO.'

'EO?'

'Michael Jackson. Even you must have heard of him.'

'Course. Bad! Is he here?'

'Don't be an idiot. It's a film.'

'Big deal,' said Emma, who had watched Justine's video of Michael Jackson back home, more times than she could remember.

'Not any old film. You wait, I've read about it.'

Breathless, they were among the last in the theatre. The music was deafening and Michael strutted his stuff in some weird space adventure. It was in 3-D and the audience had to wear special glasses. Hands reached out to grab them, people cringed as the villain leered into their faces, and it was just as if these gigantic figures were there, real in the cinema. Emma had never seen anything like it. No wonder it was on the Journey into Imagination section.

'Wow! That was brill,' said Emma.

'Better meet your folks,' said Josh, pointing to his watch. 'It's gone twelve-thirty.'

They ran to the restaurant where Dad had already ordered piles of salad covered in a creamy dressing.

'Why don't you go on the computers with me, after lunch, Emma?' asked Danny.

'Don't you want to see other things? There's lots more.'

'No. I want to do the ComminiCore. It says here,' said Danny, jabbing the guide book, 'that you can take a "firsthand look at current technological triumphs and experience tomorrow's communications systems".'

'How exciting,' said Emma, sarcastically.

'Or, there's a history of computers, and robotics. Go on, Emma, please.'

'I don't like computers.' Emma tried to ignore the look on Danny's face. 'Me and Josh have got Energy, Horizons, Motion and the Land to do yet.'

'And Spaceship Earth,' added Josh.

'So I don't want to,' she emphasised. 'I don't have to, do I Mum?' Emma wailed, convinced she would be told to stay with her brother.

Mum looked at Dad and sighed. 'No,' she said reluctantly. 'Dad's got to do Danny's physio . . .'

'Not here,' hissed Danny.

'No, in the restrooms, the toilets, so you two may as well go off. Be back at Spaceship Earth at four o'clock. We'll go on that together and then go back to the apartment for a rest,' she said.

'A rest?' asked Josh, as he and Emma raced off. 'Who needs a rest?'

'Danny. The heat gets to him and his chest.'

'So you all have to rest? Because of him?'

'Yes,' stated Emma. Having rests had been part of Danny's life for as long as she could remember. Of course he had to go slowly, or he would be really ill again.

'Well, that's not fair! Hurry up, the line-up for Horizons is moving.'

As Emma sat in their vehicle going through a journey into the twenty-first century, her mind seemed to split into two. One half soaked up the wonders displayed on the gigantic screens wrapped around her, and took in the details of the possible future habitats. She quite fancied living in a working ocean colony. Could watch fish all day.

The other half of her mind set off on another journey, sparked off by Josh's remark. It's not fair, she thought, why should Danny stop me doing things? He always does. Everything revolves round him, his physio, his tablets, his stupid chest not working properly, his hospital appointments, more of his physio, his tiredness, even his interest in football. It's not fair! What about me? Who cares about me, and what I want? It's Danny this, and Danny that, never Emma! Anger bubbled away inside her.

'You all right?' said Josh. 'Your face has gone all funny. You're never sick on that little ride!'

'No, I'm fine.' With an effort she rearranged her face. If only she had a brother like Josh, who could run, and fight, and do just about anything.

The image of Danny's pinched, pleading face at lunchtime flashed unbidden into her mind. Even the life-sized moving dinosaurs in Energy would not budge it. She felt a rush of tenderness. How could she feel so much love and so much anger at the same time? Why? Why was Danny ill? Why *her* brother? And where in all this was God? It was all right for Mum to go on about God's love, and Jesus, and going to church. If God was so great, then why hadn't he stopped Danny being ill? What had Mum said back in February? Something about if God could give them a holiday, he could keep Danny infection-free while they were away. Well, if he could do that, then why couldn't he keep Danny infection-free always? Why couldn't he make his lungs normal and all the other bits that were wrong with him? Why?

Emma rubbed her head trying to erase her thoughts. What was the matter with her? She had had no trouble, until now, believing in God, going to church when she felt like it, talking to him and just accepting that Danny was Danny. Full stop. But now! If she was honest, she was cross with God. He did not need to let Danny have CF.

In desperation Emma abandoned her thoughts as the

family drove back to the apartment after taking the dramatic ride through Spaceship Earth. The twins were in the pool and she could not face their constant chatter and inane remarks about Grandad's revolting habits.

She and Josh watched TV, switching back and forwards through the thirty-six channels. They even had one channel that did weather reports all the time. Danny had a sleep, Mum wrote postcards and Dad cooked tea. Well, he opened some tins and heated the contents up to make spaghetti surprise, the surprise being that there was no spaghetti in it!

Back at Epcot, with Angie and Leroy joining them for the evening, they stayed together, moving at a snail's pace, oohing and aahing at every exhibit. Mum insisted they watch a Disney show, so Emma prepared to be bored as Mickey and Minnie Mouse and friends, all dressed in silver space suits, danced away.

They got members of the audience to join them, always pretty girls or little kids who were too young to know how to dance and who sucked their thumbs. They never chose Emma. Who ever did? But Danny, lost in the depths of his wheelchair, got a special visit from the Mouse himself, who twirled the chair round and round, dancing with it. Trust Danny!

'Ten minutes to the fireworks. Let's get a good spot. Charge!' Dad was off, using the chair as a battering ram to get them the best view of the lakeside spectacular. Behind them the globe of Spaceship Earth was lit up an icy-blue, while in front lay the inky-black waters of the lake.

Lights dimmed. Classical music blasted out. Fountains shot into the air lit up by innumerable fireworks. They moved in time to the music, dancing in the night sky, curving, wheeling, twisting like sparkling jewels on a bed of black velvet.

Green lazer beams pulsated as far as they could see, carving up the night sky like crazy paving. Drumming to the deep beat they intertwined with the bursting fireworks. The golden, green light bathed everyone's faces in a ghostly glow.

'I thought they'd do that,' said Dad, as the stirring sounds of the 1812 Overture rang through the air.

'See that . . . and that . . .' People, heads craning upwards, watched with fascination as fireworks exploded into huge, chrysanthemum shapes while cannons boomed out. Dad started singing the tune along with lots of others, until the grand finale when firework after firework illuminated the sky with the last cannon's blast.

Spontaneous applause echoed round the lake.

'I'll say this, Leroy,' said Dad, 'you Americans really know how to put on a show! Enjoy it, Em?'

Emma was dumbstruck for once. She had wanted it to last forever. It had been magnificent, perfect, an ideal end to a magical day.

Chapter Eight

It was already Thursday and there were so many more things to see and do, yet it was a rest day again. Angie and Leroy were visiting a huge shopping mall. Mum and Emma went along with them, trailing Josh who had been promised a milkshake if he did not moan.

Even in a T-shirt Leroy looked like a bear, grey hairs sprouting out of his neckline. 'Well, girls,' he said, making Mum giggle, 'where to first?'

The mall was immense, sprawling all over the place. From the centre, spokes radiated out, lined with every sort of shop imaginable.

'Well, I want some souvenirs, and presents for back home, and you've saved up for trainers, haven't you, Emma?'

'Yes, they're a lot cheaper here.'

'Trainers?' said Leroy. 'I reckon me and the boy will skip that one.' For some reason Josh had gone bright red. 'We'll see you back here in half an hour.'

Angie led the way, passing lots of shops to reach a department store.

'But I want to look in those shops,' Emma protested.

'When you've gotten your trainers, hon,' said Angie. 'Now what size are you?'

'About a five.'

'Five? I don't rightly know what that is in American.'

'It says on the soles usually,' Mum said. 'Thirty-something.'

'Soles? I reckon I'm getting confused. Perhaps we'll work it out. Look, here they are.'

Rows of underwear! Pants and bras! Angie picked up a camisole type bra top. 'I think this will be okay. You're not that big yet.'

'What's she doing?' Emma asked Mum.

'Search me!' Mum turned to Angie. 'She wanted trainers, not these.'

'These *are* trainers. For young girls.' Angie looked at their puzzled faces. 'Oh, my, what did you mean?'

'You know, trainers, running shoes, sports things. For my feet!' Emma explained.

'Feet!' Angie collapsed with laughter. 'I thought it was for, well, this!' She pointed to her rounded bust. 'You mean sneakers for your feet!'

'No wonder Leroy and Josh disappeared!' Mum thought it hilarious but Emma could not see anything remotely funny. Any idiot knew what a pair of trainers was. Josh must think she was nuts.

After insisting on telling and retelling the story to Leroy and Josh, they found the trainers. Honestly, thought Emma, they're worse than the twins going on and on. Mum insisted on comparing prices in all the shops just in case they were cheaper anywhere else. They weren't and soon Emma was the proud owner of designer trainers.

'A coffee,' said Leroy, 'then I thought you folks were off to the Space Center.'

'No, that's tomorrow. It's mall and pool today.'

Mum joined them, a bag full of T-shirts over her arm. 'I thought we'd get a T-shirt for everyone. What do you think, Emma?'

'Fine,' said Emma. Actually it was too late to say anything. Mum had bought a pile and was spreading them out over the table so they could all have a look. What Irene Watkins, plump as a ripe cherry, was going to look like back in Birmingham, in a purple T-shirt with Minnie Mouse waving on it, was too hard to visualise.

Angie had unobtrusively made her purchases. A designer dress which cost the earth, some gold-coloured neckchains, and a pair of Italian leather sandals. Josh had a sports top and a hand-held video game.

It must be wonderful to be rich, thought Emma. You could buy whatever you wanted. In fact being American must be great. She could not imagine Angie down at the local playschool or Leroy at a car factory.

'What's he do?' she nudged Josh.

'Oh, him, he's got his own business, designs things. Mum was his sort of secretary, but she doesn't do much secretarying now!'

In fact his mum spent the rest of the day by the pool. Emma and Josh exhausted the fitness room, played tennis and swam. Dad was reading all about the Kennedy Space Center and told everyone how he could remember watching the first moon-landing on his parents old black and white TV way back in 1969.

As the Fisher family drove to the Space Center the next morning, Emma pretended that she was rich. Her fantasy lasted throughout the smooth journey. She could soon get used to this lifestyle!

They drove through the flat, green countryside, covered in low trees with the occasional, bewildered palm sticking up amongst them. A long, straight causeway led them through miles of marshy ground to the Spaceport. They spotted wild alligators, like half-submerged tree trunks, lazily paddling in the shallow pools. Long-legged white birds, ibis and egrets, picked their way through the scrubby undergrowth, moving their feet so carefully that they looked as if they were trying to avoid something unmentionable underfoot.

'We'll look at the shuttle and the rockets before we take the tour. Danny, if you use your chair round the exhibits, you needn't have it on the tour.' Dad was looking forward to this visit. He photographed everything.

Each day Dad looked more like a tourist, wandering around armed with guidebooks and taking photographs at every opportunity. He wore shorts all the time and his legs were getting sunburnt. Emma thought he looked daft as he was white from the ankles down because he kept sneaking his socks on, despite her protests.

'Mark, it's late. I'm starving. Let's have a snack before the tour. There's something called the Lunch Pad. That'll do.'

'Burgers,' said Danny.

'Hot dog, apple cake, Coke.' Emma gave her order. 'What about Danny's physio?'

Dad looked peeved. 'You'll last out until after the tour, won't you? It takes two hours.' Funny how he could be flexible about the physio when it was him who desperately wanted to see something.'

'Course, Dad. Can we go in the shop? And there's a film.'

'After the tour.'

The two hours sped by. They were directed in and

out of their air-conditioned coach, the guide explaining as they went. The Center covered one hundred and forty thousand acres and was a wildlife reserve, although how bald-headed eagles got on with the business of nesting while tourists trundled past and rockets occasionally blasted off, was a mystery.

'This is where all the Apollo astronauts trained. Please exit the bus, enter the door immediately ahead, and afterwards join the bus at the other side of the building.'

The dark hangar was dimly lit as Emma stumbled along the walkway. She leaned on the railing as the spotlight picked out an army man who looked like something straight off a film set. He told them all about the moon landing. Dad was rapt and even Emma felt a strange tingle in her spine when the lights went up on a weird golden and silver structure that looked like an attempt at modern art that had gone wrong.

'This is an actual Apollo lunar module. Flash photography is allowed at this juncture.'

Dad went camera mad. 'Just think, to the moon in that!'

'It's so small,' said Danny. 'Looks like it'll fall to pieces.'

Dramatic music accompanied the dimming of lights, as a sense of awe enveloped the gawping tourists. Then it was on to see the launch pads, to watch a simulated space lift-off, to view the crawler that weighed six million pounds.

'These,' said the guide, 'carry the space shuttles to their launch pads. It takes eight hours to cover three miles on the specially strengthened road which has foundations over six feet deep.' He seemed to appreciate the 'oohs' from his coachload. 'Now, if you get out at the next stop you can inspect a Saturn rocket. It's as long as one of your soccer fields,' he said to Danny, 'and you can take photos of the vehicle assembly plant, one of the biggest buildings in the world.'

'They're proud of the size of everything, aren't they Dad?' said Danny, as he stood dwarfed by the Saturn rocket.'

'They've got cause to be. Imagine this in space. It's fantastic.'

'But they do go on about how wonderful America is 'cos they did all this,' Emma chipped in, waving her arm expansively.

'It's a different culture, that's all,' said Dad. 'We British tend to underplay our achievements, but the Americans are proud of who they are and what they've done.'

'Is that why some of the houses have American flags outside?' asked Emma.

'Expect so. Are you okay to walk round this rocket, Danny?'

'Course,' said Danny, whose legs felt as strong as wet string. No way was he going to let on that he could tell he needed to do his chest physio. For two hours he could pretend to be like anyone else. Fortunately Dad was so interested in the Center that he did not notice Danny getting weaker all the time.

Back at base, Mum did his physio in the boiling hot car while Dad bought himself a NASA T-shirt, a mug and some superb prints taken from space.

'Time for the film,' he said. 'It says you can see the world as you've never seen it before, its awesome fury, dazzling beauty, and it's the closest thing to going into space without riding the shuttle.'

The guide book was not exaggerating. On a screen

as high as a five and a half storey building, they joined astronauts in pre-flight training, on a breathtaking launch, as they circuited the world and dangled outside the shuttle in space, and as they made a death-defying landing.

Emma felt very small, very insignificant. From the spacecraft the world looked so little. Half of Italy in one shot on the screen, the Middle East crossed in seconds. She could see coastlines, major river mouths, smudges of dark colours which must be mountains. It was so beautiful, so fragile. And yet down there were hundreds of millions of people all scurrying about, busy as ants, living out their separate lives.

She held up her hand to her eyes and blocked out a quarter of a continent. Just like that. Emma felt alone in the hushed, crowded cinema. The world had always seemed so big. Even Birmingham was vast, let alone England or the Atlantic or Florida. Yet it wasn't big at all.

No wonder she felt strange. If God's up there somewhere even higher than the spacecraft, she thought, it's hardly surprising that he can't hear me ask him to make Danny better. I expect he can't see much at all, only the shapes and maybe the blocks of sprawling cities.

She glanced at her brother who was worn out. His face was so tired that he looked like an old man. Emma resisted the urge to reach out and hold his hand. He would wonder what was up with her.

The film zoomed in, hurtling them through space, faster and faster, picking out details, as the astronauts prepared to land. She could see the surf pounding along the coast, the white ribbon of sand, greenery, individual trees and then the final touch down on the sunbaked airstrip.

Perhaps God was more like that. Perhaps he had a zoom-like quality that could home in on details of life on earth. After all, Mum often said that God loved and cared for them all. But how could he do that if he did not know what was happening? Dad never said anything. Emma wondered what he thought.

'Dad,' she said as the film finished, 'do you think God's up there?'

He smiled. 'That's your mum's department.' He would not give a straight answer. Emma did not want to ask Mum. She knew what she would say.

'If you are up there, God, please do something about Danny,' she said quietly, gazing into the cloudless sky. 'I can understand if you can't hear me but I do hope you can.'

'Emma,' Mum called. 'We're going into the souvenir shop again. Your dad's crazy about this place.'

Emma jumped. She did not want Mum asking her what she was doing talking into space. 'Okay. I'll be at the art exhibition.'

As she looked at the paintings, Emma felt a sense of peace. All this beauty, this wonder. Surely God was real after all. It could not have just happened. It was too marvellous.

Chapter Nine

Saturday dawned hot and airless. Another perfect day, ideal for Typhoon Lagoon, a water park in Disneyworld, where Mum mistakenly thought they could have a quiet, relaxing day. What a hope! Admittedly there was some sunbathing, but it was punctuated by sharp bursts of activity for them all except Danny.

'I'm going in the lagoon first,' he said.

'No, Danny.'

'But, Dad . . .'

'It's too rough for you. That tidal wave that comes every ninety seconds will knock you to bits'

'But, Dad, you can help me.' Danny was near to tears, looking even smaller in his bathing trunks and baseball cap.

'I'm sorry, Danny, no. I can't risk it. It knocks the breath out of anyone, let alone . . .' he floundered to a halt.

'Let alone a wimp like me. I'll stay just in the shallow bit by the little kids. Please! Mum, go on, make him.'

'No!' Dad was getting cross. If only the others would disappear he could deal with his son. 'I'll tell you what, I'll push you round and we can see what there is.'

'See!' screeched Danny. 'I don't want to *see*. I want

to *do*. Do.' He burst into tears, his skinny chest bones protruding like a skeleton's, heaving away.

Mum took charge. 'Angie, why don't you take the kids to the lagoon. Mark, take Leroy and have a drink. I'll deal with this.' Obediently they left, slow-footed, quietly, while Danny continued to rage on, his sobs only partly muffled by his mum's enfolding arms.

'Does he usually do this?' asked Josh.

'No,' said Emma. 'Never. Let's float in the lagoon.' She fell silent. It must be awful, all this water, twisting slides, raging rapids, high speed chutes and not to be able to go on any of it. No wonder Danny was throwing a fit.

Thanks a lot, God, she thought angrily. So much for listening to me at the Space Center! Fat lot of good that did! She half expected Danny to sprout muscles, grow a few inches and lose his cough overnight. I mean, she thought, if you could raise people from the dead when Jesus was on earth, why don't you do something about my brother? Surely that would be easier than making someone alive again. She'd give up on God. After all he had given up on her.

Angie drifted next to her and held her hand as the tidal wave surged towards them. Everyone screamed as the powerful surf pushed their bodies forwards as if they were spent matchsticks in an old puddle. Emma felt herself go under, her arms and legs flailed wildly and she surfaced, blinking into the harsh sunlight, laughing as water streamed off her face.

'That was sure nice what the folks did back home,' said Angie, who managed to look like the front of a magazine even when dripping wet. Her golden hair was covered in a bright scarf that matched her bikini exactly.

Even her eye make-up had not smudged. It must be expensive. Mum usually looked like a panda, with smudged mascara, whether she was wet or dry.

'Did what?' said Emma, waiting for the next wave.

'You know, give you the holiday, with Danny being so . . .' She changed tack. 'Some church you guys go to!'

'Yes,' replied Emma, at a loss for what to say. 'Some church.' And some God too, said a little voice. He might not have come up trumps with Danny, but the holiday! Thousands of pounds, she'd seen the prices in the brochure, and all the spending money. However she looked at it, God was involved in that somehow.

It was like one of those equations they tried to do at school. A plus B equals C. Just think, her class was probably doing them right now. A, a God who gave them a fabulous holiday, plus B, a God who let Danny have CF, and have it so badly his lungs were no good, equalled C. Emma had not got a clue what C was.

'I'll never understand God,' she said aloud, not realising she was speaking.

'What did you say?' Josh bobbed next to her, his silvery teeth brace glinting in the sunlight.

'Nothing.' Emma decided to abandon the God equation and get on with living. 'Let's line up for the chutes.'

The hours slid into each other. Avoiding going back to Mum and Danny, the others rode the waves, clung onto huge, inflated rings as they spun down the rapids, and screamed as they plunged off the end of chutes into foamy water.

Everywhere there were lifeguards, tanned, young and fit, wearing bright red swimming costumes and hollering 'Keep away from the sides,' or 'One at a time now'.

They had floats attached to them and there was a bit of excitement when one of them dived into the lagoon. The tidal wave had just reached its highest point and perched on top of it was Dad's Captain Florida hat, but no Dad.

'He must have thought you'd gone under,' said Mum, as they related the incident.

'I felt such a fool,' said Dad. 'I'd climbed in my ring and got stuck. The hat went one way, me the other.'

'I'm glad I wasn't with you,' said Emma. Trust Dad to show them up.

Danny was back to normal. No-one mentioned the earlier tantrum. 'I'm starving,' he said.

Angie and Leroy had insisted on bringing a picnic and Emma was thankful that Mum had not argued with them. Chicken legs, quiche, salads, four different kinds of cake, huge grapes and Coke by the gallon emerged from a cool box the size of a small fridge.

'You certainly know how to do these things,' said Dad, waving a chicken leg in one hand and a wedge of cheese in the other. 'Better than your efforts, eh, Sue?' He missed his wife's warning look. 'I think if I saw another doorstep sandwich again, I'd turn into one.'

'Sunbathing time,' said Mum, ignoring him. 'And afterwards I thought we'd all take Danny on the Lazy River.'

Over-eager agreement met this suggestion, and at last Mum declared that lunch was safely digested. She had already done the physio and it was time for the Lazy River.

The circular river gently wafted them along as they sat, bottoms wedged into their inflatable rings. It wound its way all round the park and the lagoon, through a rainfall, rock tunnels, by steamy tropics, past banks of bright flowers and under rustic bridges. Yellow butterflies, with wings as big as a child's hand, sipped elegantly from the flowers.

'This is ace,' said Danny, secure in the calm water. There was no danger of getting knocked about here. In his over-sized T-shirt to stop him getting too sunburnt, he looked like anyone else. Nobody actually said anything but it just worked out that one of them stayed with him for the rest of the time, completing innumerable circuits in the warm water.

Leroy took Josh and Emma to have a go at snorkelling. He eased his vast body into the wet suit jacket while Emma put hers on. It felt cold and clammy despite the heat of the day. They were given instructions on how to use the snorkels and masks. Gently they lowered themselves, face first into the water.

Emma gasped, water shooting up her nostrils. It was so cold! And salty! It had not occurred to her that the fish she would be snorkelling among would be in salt water, artificially lowered to sea temperature. She spluttered about until the instructor sorted her out, and she was off.

At first it took all Emma's concentration to keep breathing correctly as she swam, only her bottom and a bit of the back of her head showing above the water. As she got the hang of it, she watched in wonder as beautiful shiny fish carefully swam back and forward. Reaching down her hands, some tiny fish glided through her fingers. Seaweed waved to her from the bottom of the pool and a big long grey fish eyed her glassily from his lair, deep beneath her. Blues, reds, oranges, sparkling colours and she was swimming amongst them!

Too soon it was over and Leroy jogged them off to the lagoon again, his belly bouncing above his swimming shorts, as if it had a life of its own. Actually he was not that bad. He could not help being old and Emma could understand why he treated Angie like a rare and precious jewel. Would anyone ever treat her like that, she wondered. If she took after Mum she would hardly be the glamorous type. Mind you, even Mum was looking pretty good after a week in the sun and wearing some decent clothes.

'I'll join Danny,' she called. 'See you later.'

Half asleep, she lay back in her tube holding Danny's hand so that the two tubes formed a figure eight.

'This is brill!' said Danny. 'Isn't it Em?'

'Sure.'

'I want it to go on forever.'

'Me too.'

'Except I'll miss City's home games.'

'You and your football. You're worse than Dad!' she said.

'*Better* you mean. Hey, look! Clouds. They're whoppers.'

'Um,' Emma was tired. 'Shush a bit. I'm resting.' She floated lazily on, the warm sun turning her face deep gold. This was fantastic. This was what life was all about.

As the clouds in the sky massed away to the east, a thought struck Emma. I'm having the best time of my life, but it's only because Danny is ill.

She sat up, capsized the tube, spluttered upright, grabbed Danny and continued on her journey.

We'd never have been given this holiday if Danny wasn't bad, she thought. A strange, unknown feeling crept over her. It was a bit like the time she had been caught pinching crisps from the school tuck shop. It was weird and uncomfortable. It was guilt.

How could she, how could Mum and Dad enjoy themselves so much with Danny so . . . so ill she supposed? It wasn't fair. She would give anything, absolutely anything, to make Danny better. She would never moan when she was asked to do jobs. She would work hard at school and even learn her French. She would go to church twice on Sundays and become a nun, if it helped, but nothing made any difference. It was so unfair. Danny was such a nice kid. Why did it have to be him that was ill?

'Evacuate the water areas! Evacuate! Thunderstorm approaching!'

Emma grabbed Danny and tried to hurry him to the nearest way out of the Lazy River. Mum was clucking around like a demented hen as the sky darkened and thundered ominously.

'Hurry up!'

'I am,' Emma half-pushed Danny up the steps and into his chair.

'Quick, let's shelter.' Lightning crackled across the sky competing with the 'Evacuate the pool' announcements.

'Get to the shelter. Hurry.'

'But I'm wet already, and it's still boiling hot.' Emma followed her mum.

'It's the lightning. It's dangerous with the water.' Mum was upset, unable to hide her fear. And then it started to rain, and rain, and rain. Thunder, flashes, crackles, drumming water.

'The park will not re-open today! Not re-open,' said the loudspeakers as rain deluged down. Soaked, they ran for the cars, Dad carrying Danny, Leroy heaving the cool box and their clothes all piled up on the chair. Overhead the sky rivalled Disney's display at Epcot. Emma had never seen anything like it.

'No wonder the grass is so green,' said Dad. 'I wondered why.'

'It's not fair,' said Emma, longing for the Lazy River.

'Things aren't,' said Dad, in a voice that made Emma think he was talking about more than thunderstorms.

It was true. Life wasn't fair. Emma could run and splash and have fun for hours. Danny could not. She took it for granted, like the hot dry weather. Now the rain had spoilt it. She hadn't wanted today, this Saturday, to end like this. Life was so confusing!

Chapter Ten

Being confused was too much like hard work, thought Emma. The best thing to do was to stop thinking and to get on with enjoying herself. Today was another rest day. Actually Emma did not mind. Josh always seemed to be around and the pool was ace.

'Hi, Emma, come and play leapfrog.'

'In the pool! Darlene, you're nuts.'

'I'm Cindy. Yes, in the pool. Do you know my grandad . . .'

'Our grandad,' interrupted the real Darlene.

'Once took us out in a boat.'

'And it turned over.'

'And we were rescued.'

'By the coastguard, with lifejackets.'

'Us, not him. We had the lifejackets,' said Cindy. 'So Grandma said no boats this trip.'

'She also said Grandad was a silly old . . .'

'You're not to say that word, Darlene, even though he is.'

'Is what?' Emma was bemused.

'A silly old . . . well . . . wotsit.'

Josh strolled into the pool area. Emma was relieved. She could not take any more of the double act.

'Pool?' queried Josh.

Emma propelled him away towards the fitness room. 'Not with them two in it. I wish they would wear different costumes. I can't tell them apart. Do you think they exist?'

'Who?'

'Grandma and Grandad.'

'Course,' Josh pointed to a balcony. 'They spy out the land from up there. You can see them.'

They looked very ordinary, not much older than Leroy. They waved at the children and promised cookies later on.

'Let's have a race on the exercise bikes,' said Emma, entering the fitness room.

Hot and tired after their exertions, they returned to the poolside and put up with the twins' chatter as they enjoyed Grandma's cookies. Mum, Dad and Danny joined them, and Mum was amazed that Grandma baked on holiday. Mum hardly ever baked.

'I'll do you folks one of my specials. You'll join us tonight? Grand.'

When Mum protested that it was a lot of work for her, Grandad insisted that she enjoyed it and if Mum would keep an eye on the twins, he would drive his wife to the supermarket.

'Don't rush,' said Mum. 'We'll be here all day. Why not lunch out? I'll see to the girls.'

'Well, thanks, I reckon we will!' and he was off.

Mum was to regret her words. The twins found Josh and Emma an uninterested audience, so told Mum all the details of their lives. Ranging from their birth, which they knew an awful lot about, through school, friends, detailed descriptions of their home, why Grandad had a long scar on his arm, holidays they had had, on and on they went.

Even when Mum fell asleep they continued, unperturbed by her lack of interest. Josh rescued Danny from their clutches, inflated the replacement air bed, and trundled him around the pool. The twins started to join them, so Josh went deeper into the water.

'You mustn't come close. You might splash him. He's ill.' Josh turned to Danny. 'I hope you don't mind me using you as an excuse.'

Danny grinned. 'Use away! They're driving me nuts. I'll be as ill as you like today. Later on I will need some peace and quiet and you and Em can come up to the apartment and play the football game.'

'I don't know which is worse, them or football,' laughed Emma. 'I think I'll have a bit of both.'

By the time of the evening meal they were all on good terms. Emma and Josh had invented lots of stories about their families to stem the torrent from the twins. During the meal Cindy reached out and stroked Emma's dad's legs. He ignored her.

'It's true,' she whispered. 'It *is* hairy. Wow! We sure don't have artificial legs like that in the States.'

'Don't touch his chest,' said Emma. 'He doesn't like people to know he has a steel rib cage from when he was shot down over Germany in the war.'

The twins looked at him, goggle-eyed. Dad had not been born in the war, let alone shot down. Their maths must be hopeless to not work that out.

'Now, don't talk,' said Danny, 'or he'll have one of his rages. He goes purple and green, swells up and roars like a lion.'

'What are you lot whispering about?' asked Dad.

'Nothing,' replied a twin. 'I'm hot.'

'Turn the air-conditioning up, Grandad,' called Grandma.

'Anything to oblige, ma'am,' he teased her. The whirring noise got louder.

'Aagh!' screamed Emma. 'Get it off! Help!'

A huge shiny cockroach had been blown out of the vent above her and had landed in her lap.

'It's only a little one,' said Grandad, calmly removing it. 'They live in the vents. I'm surprised you've not had any in your apartment.'

Emma mentally vowed to shut off her bedroom vents. The creature was revolting.

Dad tried to shift attention away from the unfortunate insect. 'These steaks are ace. Have you been to the MGM studios yet?'

'Did it last Monday,' said Grandad, and proceeded to tell them all about it. 'You folks going tomorrow? Monday's a good day. Not so crowded.'

Monday was brill, let alone good. Emma kicked up a bit of a fuss because Josh could not join them. Leroy was taking him and Angie to meet an old aunt who lived in one of the many retirement villages in Florida. Josh was not impressed.

The Disney MGM studios were the newest attraction in Disneyworld and Danny could see or go on anything he wanted to. It was hard to tell which was the best thing. Danny loved the stunt spectacular, where stunt men charged around, blowing things up, leaping out of buildings and overturning runaway trucks.

Mum, meanwhile, went all nostalgic during the great movie ride. When Danny had been younger and off school ill, he and Mum had watched a lot of old black and white films on the TV. She knew them all and started retelling the stories until everyone told her to be quiet.

'We'll do special effects, then lunch, physio and the backstage tour,' declared Dad. 'We've a fair bit of walking but the chair can go anywhere.' Danny was half-buried under cameras, drinks, leaflets and Mum's cardigan, although why she wanted it with her in ninety degree heat was a mystery. He also held onto Dad's special bag with the money, cheque cards and tickets in it. Dad would not let it out of his sight.

Everything was so real. The ocean storm scene re-created in a water tank looked like a raging typhoon when shown on the video screen. They watched artists creating cartoons, following the progress from story idea, through animation, effects, painting each picture, which was called a cel, to the final editing and screening.

'All that work,' said Dad, 'to produce one bit of film!'

'Makes you hungry,' said Danny.

'Not pizza again,' Mum sighed.

'Okay, Sue, let's make it burgers. You can always have a salad.'

After lunch Dad and Danny disappeared for half an hour's physio while Emma roamed around. She really felt as if she was in the streets of New York, or outside a real mansion although it was only painted board. Old cars and props out of recent films studded the area. No wonder films made everything seem so real.

The backstage tour was on a shuttle bus. They rode past a 'hot' set where filming was actually happening. No-one wanted them for extras though.

'Please be warned, you may get wet whilst experiencing Catastrophe Canyon.'

A gate opened into a desert canyon complete with rocky outcrops, an old road tanker and an atmosphere of forthcoming disaster.

The shuttle bus rocked as the ground heaved. The tanker slid towards them and erupted into flames, just before a wall of water from a burst dam threatened to engulf them all in its flailing depths. Emma could feel the heat of the explosions, smell the acrid smoke of the blazing tanker, feel the spray of the water. For a few moments she was there, either about to drown or about to burst into flame.

The rocking ceased, the tanker slid back up the hill, the fires went out, the water disappeared and the shuttle bus continued its tour.

'Look,' said Danny, as they passed the back of the canyon. 'It's all a set.' Scaffolding, water pipes, warning notices, the skeleton of the huge structure were already vibrating as the next shuttle load of tourists were treated to their own catastrophe.

After the excitement of that, they worked their way round the other exhibits.

'Everything's so professional,' commented Mum. 'All the details. Those Muppets were amazing.'

'And the Star Tours!' said Emma. 'I really thought I was flying through space in an intergalactic war.'

'Don't!' shuddered Mum. 'Those simulator rides are too much for me. I forget I'm just sitting there. I really think all the things that are happening are real.'

'Perhaps they are,' said Dad.

'You what?' Emma was puzzled.

'Perhaps all this,' he spread his hands expansively, 'is reality, and Birmingham, the factory, that window-cleaning round I want to do, perhaps all that is pretend.'

'Mark, don't be so daft,' said Mum.

'Well, don't you wish it were so?' Dad looked sad.

'You know how I feel.' Mum had her 'let's all look on the bright side' voice in operation, which did not fool anyone.

'Come on,' said Emma. 'There's a show over there. Starts in five minutes, and you know we're supposed to be early with the chair. Run.' She did not like all this talk of reality.

Disney characters saluted all the well known Hollywood stars in a glamorous musical show. If only this were reality, thought Emma. If only we could stay here forever. I could go to school. We could live in the apartment. Danny could play in the pool every day. We could visit Josh in Chicago and even the twins in Colorado. Mum would always look pretty and happy, like today, and Dad would never be grumpy and go on about not having enough money. Only a few days left, just until Saturday.

The dancers stopped, lights went on and they moved on to the next show. That was what life was like. This holiday was like a show and they would have to move on, but there would not be another spectacular to excite and delight them. Just Birmingham, school, CF, the factory. Just reality.

Well, whatever happens, thought Emma as they stopped for Dad to reload the camera with its seventh film, nothing can take all this away from me. I'm in Florida, in Disneyworld. I've been on everything, done everything. No-one can take that away from me!

Chapter Eleven

Danny was very tired the next morning. He had weird dreams all night long in which he changed from space commander to monster, then to dancing pig, all whilst music swirled around. The dreams had woken him up and he had had one of his coughing bouts.

'Too much mental stimulation, my lad,' said Mum, as Danny recounted the dreams. 'You need a quiet day in bed.'

'Not bed!'

'Well, lounger by the pool then. Your chest could be the backing beat for a pop group.'

'Aw, mum,' protested Danny. 'Can I watch TV?'

'Of course. Emma, you'd better get ready.'

Emma was fed up. 'For the pool! Grief, I can do that with my eyes closed. I want to . . .'

'Shut up a minute and listen. That nice Leroy said you could join him, Angie and Josh at some water-hole. I said you could go, so get a change of clothes and,' Mum's voice got louder as Emma dashed off, 'don't forget the suntan oil.'

'What about me?' protested Danny. 'I want to go.'

'Well, you can't. Let Emma go off without making a fuss.'

'She's always going off!'

'It's my life,' called Emma, grabbing a clean towel. 'See you,' and she went to Josh's apartment. Fancy Mum arranging for her to spend the day with Josh's family! Things were looking up.

After leaving the car in one of the huge parking lots, they boarded a coach that took them through thick, wooded country to a lake-side area.

'Last bus back, five-thirty, folks,' said the driver.

Emma was glad Danny was not with them. No folded wheelchair, no pitying looks, no fuss helping him down the steps or across the pathways, no interfering old ladies, and it was always old ones, asking what was the matter with him. Just her and Josh. Today she would pretend to be Emma Everett, not Fisher. She could start by copying the accent.

'The water-hole first?' she queried.

'Pardon?'

'Water-hole.'

Josh laughed. 'I can't tell what you're saying. Let's go to the water-hole.'

Emma gave up the American accent then and there.

The water-hole was like a big bite taken out of a lake sandwich. The bite had been deepened, given jetties, slides, ropes and tyres to swing on, rocks, and an edging of sunloungers. Fit, tanned bodies leapt off ropes, soared off jetties, splash-landed down chutes and performed death-defying feats from dangling tyres.

It was a good job Danny was not there. He would have had to stay in the neat, safe children's pool and, if Typhoon Lagoon was anything to go by, he would have made a fuss. His arms were too weak to hang on to ropes and he could not run up and down the jetties.

Emma looked around. Everywhere else they had visited had had a fair number of wheelchairs but there were none here. Danny would have stuck out like a sore thumb.

Leroy was in his element. 'When I was a boy we had a place like this on the ranch.'

'You lived on a ranch?' asked Emma.

'Sure thing. My folks would go down the river and splash in the hole there. Mighty muddy it got. I recollect the time I took Misty in there. Got stuck.'

'What was Misty?' asked Josh. Not liking Leroy was getting harder to do.

'My horse. I thought he could do with cooling off. 'Bout your age at the time.'

'What happened?'

'Well, he stuck in that there mud and we couldn't budge him. My brother fetched my daddy. Man, was he mad! He roped Misty, got a tractor and dragged her out. My, was my backside sore after he paddled me.'

'Paddled you?' Emma had got lost.

'Warmed my backside with his belt. Them times were different. You kids don't know you're born.'

'Then what?' asked Josh.

'He banned us from the pool, but that didn't last long. After chores, me and my brother would creep down there. I'll show you what we played.'

To Emma's amazement he grabbed a rope swing, clambered up it, like an orang-utan, swung himself gently, let out a wild yell and dived head first into the water.

A whistle rang out sharply, as a lifeguard sprang into action and lectured the 'great ape' on irresponsible behaviour in the water.

'Well, at least he didn't paddle me,' said Leroy, who seemed to have found the whole incident amusing.

'You're a bad influence on the kids.' Angie, who had no intention of getting wet today, put her magazine down. 'Now, don't shake all that water over me. Go and play!'

'Sound like they're already married,' whispered Emma to Josh, as Leroy obediently trotted off, unrepentant. He took them on the water chutes, played tag on and under the jetties and tried unsuccessfully to ride astride a bucking oil drum anchored in the water.

'Did you ride horses a lot?' asked Emma, as he attempted to hold her on the oil-drum.

'Eight to ten hours a day when we were herding cattle. Course, school days we'd be lucky to get two or three hours in the saddle after helping in the stables and yard.'

'Why aren't you there now?' asked Josh. The Leroy he knew was a big city man.

'It's a long story. Maybe I'll take you and your mum out to the ranch one day. My brother runs it now. Like that?'

'Great. And can I go in the water-hole?'

'Sure. Now lunch. We'll have Mexican.'

Whatever was in the food, it nearly took the roof off Emma's mouth but she said nothing as the others calmly ate it as if it was as mild as mashed potato. The afternoon passed quickly as they splashed around the water hole.

They just made it to the last bus and drove home, worn out by hours of swimming and leaping about. Only Angie was fresh and full of energy after lying half-asleep on a lounger all day. Emma staggered to the apartment and collapsed onto a chair in the shade of the balcony.

Her long, firm legs stretched out in front of her, golden as melted butter, the tiny hairs bleached white by the sun. Her bare feet were criss-crossed with white marks from her sandal straps and her nose was beginning to peel.

Idly, she pulled at a fragment of transparent, loose skin and sank back further into the chair. She was nearly asleep when a familiar voice buzzed slowly into her consciousness. It was Mum, talking to Dad just centimetres away inside the apartment.

'At least he's got to today without being bad. I think the extra sleep will have done him good. The physio took ages to clear his chest.'

'Good job Emma was out of the way. She gets upset when she sees him like that,' said Dad.

I don't! thought Emma.

'Still,' continued Dad. 'Only four days left. He should make it. I've increased the antibiotics.'

'It's been great though, hasn't it Mark? I mean, he's loved every minute and it's so nice for us all to have such a wonderful break. I'm so thankful.'

'Me, too. You know, Sue, this holiday came at just the right time. Next year would have been too late.'

'You needn't tell me that, Mark Fisher.' Mum sounded sad. 'I heard the consultant last time, too, you know. I don't understand it. Lots of CF children grow into adults with little trouble, but that's not going to be the case with our Danny, not the way his lungs are damaged.'

Emma heard movement and a strangled sob noise.

'Sue, Sue. It's all right. He doesn't know and Emma has no idea. We've just got to go on as normal for however long it takes.'

Nose-blowing noises. A long silence. 'Make us a cup

of tea, Mark. I've got to pull myself together before I fetch Danny from the twins.'

'Have you noticed how they keep looking at my chest?' said Dad. 'Weird or what?'

Emma half-smiled. So the twins still believed the steel ribcage story! But what about the rest of what she had overheard. 'That's not going to be the case with Danny.' What did they mean? Danny was okay. So, he got weak and had to go to hospital, but that did not mean . . . it could not mean . . . no!

Look at Pete Withers, chairman of their local CF group, at least thirty and fitter than Danny. Or Melanie, off to University this autumn. Or Sarah, who worked as a nursery nurse. They all had CF but were okay.

But, said a little voice, what about Julia who had been buried just before Christmas, or Jim, who was fifteen and seemed to live at the hospital?

But they aren't Danny, thought Emma. It's Danny that matters, Danny. There can't ever be a time without Danny. There just can't. Without realising it, she clenched her fists and stamped her feet. Danny was the best brother anyone could wish for.

The door opened. Mum, her eyes hidden by sunglasses, was startled. 'Oh, you're there. Didn't expect you back yet.'

Obviously, thought Emma.

'Pop over to the twins and fetch Danny, will you? It's teatime.'

Emma popped. Danny walked back with her, his face alive with enthusiasm as she retold him Leroy's ranch stories. He held her hand, his sparrow-like fingers fluttering inside her strong ones.

Teatime was normal, although Emma did not feel

hungry, even though the Mexican lunch had long since been digested.

'They're showing a film down by reception,' said Danny. 'Can we go?'

'Course,' said Dad, loading the dishwasher.

'I'm tired,' said Emma. 'I'll go to bed.'

'Bed! You!' Dad looked astonished.

Mum felt her forehead. 'You seem all right. Perhaps a touch of the sun. Have a lie-down and join us later if you want.' Turning to Dad she whispered loud enough for Emma to hear. 'Leave her, Mark. Hormones, you know.'

Emma tossed and turned. 'Not the case with Danny.' Like a crazy jingle it would not leave her head. 'Not the case!' 'Danny.' In desperation she threw on her T-shirt and shorts and joined the others at the film. Anything, even a science fiction film, to black out the menacing, persistent jingle that went round and round her tired brain.

Chapter Twelve

Surprisingly, Emma slept well. After a lazy start, Dad organised them all to go off to Sea World.

'We'll buy breakfast out, late, and then spend the day there,' he said. 'There's loads to see.'

He was right. Whales and dolphins in tune with their trainers performed in deep, blue pools. Sea lions entertained them with amazing antics. They could dance, play ball, 'sing' down a microphone, mimic their trainers, and almost tease the audience. A great, brown, sea elephant leaned nonchalantly on the side of his tank. At a command, he spat volumes of water onto the audience, who loved it.

'It's time for the killer whales,' said Danny, clutching an information schedule. He had made no fuss about the wheelchair today. 'I want to sit where I can get wet. First fourteen rows.' Dad got him into position.

'I'm going further back with Mum. You two behave.'

A silent black and white figure glided menacingly in front of them across the glass walled tank. Metres of whale, killer whale, that could tear a man in pieces. The show began.

The trainers rode on the backs of the whales, dived with them, playing roly-poly, and got the mammals to leap, arching into the air. The sunlight turned the water droplets into thousands of diamonds as the graceful whales flipped back into the water. One surfaced, nose first, a trainer standing on its nose, centimetres away from ferocious teeth and certain death. It rose majestically, higher and higher, the trainer balancing, until at the top of its arch, it dived back into the water, the trainer copying its movement.

'Wow!' Danny was spellbound. 'Emma, did you see?'

'Shush, watch!'

The whales slid onto a platform and someone, not Emma of course, was chosen from the audience to sit on its back.

'We warn you that rows one through fourteen will get wet!'

Not us, thought Emma, on row twelve, but she was wrong.

A whale steamed round the edge of the tank, its huge tail, its fluke, pounding the water. With uncanny accuracy the fluke tipped the water, cold and salty, outwards over the audience.

They screamed in unison as the cold water soaked them to the skin, laughing and shouting at the same time.

'Brill!' shouted Danny. 'More.'

The whales obliged before completing some huge jumps in a grand finale.

Mum was fussing. 'You're drenched! Danny, you'll catch your death of a cold.'

Emma flinched at the phrase, but Danny solved the problem by stripping to his pants, after buying a killer whale T-shirt to change into. Emma stayed wet, the hot sun making spirals of steam curl up from her sodden clothes.

'At least we had the chair,' said Mum. 'Let's have a hot drink and then what?'

'Terrors of the Deep, a film about marine life and a water-skiing show, then the whales again.' Danny referred to his schedule.

'Only if you sit at the back.'

'Yes, Dad,' they chorused.

During the water-skiing show, Emma found herself watching Danny as much as the skiers. He was engrossed in the show, sitting forward on the chair as he watched the men and women do stunts, perform improbable cartwheels, and mass to make a wobbling pyramid. His hands steered an imaginary power boat as two of the real things fought out a duel on the lake in front of them. Plumes of water shot sky high as the boats danced through the now, choppy water. Boats and skiers combined in heart-stopping acrobatics and grinning, wetsuit clad skiers shot onto the shore, waving and smiling.

Danny cheered as loud as the rest of them. How could he? He could walk, just, but usually was bound to his wheelchair, and here he was clapping and yelling at men and women who could perform feats he could never even dream of doing. They could run and jump, somersault, fly through water in control of their well-muscled bodies and still not be breathless. Danny could walk a bit, swim a little and that was it. His body could never do all these other wonderful things and yet he did not seem to mind.

Look at him now. Eager to see the killer whales again. Only the scenes at Typhoon Lagoon, when he had so much wanted to go into the water, reminded Emma that maybe after all, her brother did mind, and minded a lot.

The whales performed in their floodlit pool weaving a web of magic over the audience. They were so beautiful, so graceful, it made Emma feel sad. She was quiet all the way home, thinking about the leaping sea creatures. Even the fish could do more than Danny.

'Emma, what's up?' Mum flopped onto the settee next to her daughter.

'Nothing.'

'Come off it. You went all quiet last night. Now tonight the same. Is something bothering you?' Emma hesitated. 'Dad's doing Danny's physio in our bedroom, so they can't hear.'

Emma struggled inside. It was like being tied up in knots and not knowing how to escape. 'Is Danny dying?' she blurted out, not daring to look at Mum. 'Is he?'

Mum gently held her hand. 'He's not well, you know that.'

'But is he *dying*?'

'No and yes,' sighed Mum. 'Danny will not live as long as most CF sufferers. His lungs are too badly damaged. We don't know how long he's got.'

'But he could get better.'

'No, Emma, there's no cure, you know that. Only a very few can have a heart-lung transplant, and that's the only hope. He'll get weaker, have more infections, and then . . .' Her voice tailed off. 'And then,' she said, with a forced smile, 'he'll be in a far better place. Do you know what, Emma?'

'What?'

'I've been thinking about this a lot this holiday. Heaven is better than Disneyworld, the Magic Kingdom, Sea World and all of Florida rolled into one.'

'Sure,' said Emma, not believing her.

'It's hard to imagine, Emma, but to be with Jesus *is* better, far better, than anything we've ever done. And you know what? In heaven Danny won't have to do his physio exercises, his legs will walk and run. Look, I'll show you.' Sniffing, she got up and took her little Bible out of her bag.

'Here, listen. This is God speaking about heaven. "There will be no more death, no more grief or crying",' tears started to run down her face. She gulped and continued, ' "or pain. The old things have disappeared".'

Emma started to cry as well. 'Why are we crying, Mum, when it says there will be no more crying?'

'I don't know. Perhaps it's because we're happy. Perhaps it's because we're sad.'

They fell silent, two statues quietly holding hands, locked in their own thoughts and grief. Emma held on to Mum, the tears just flowing down her cheeks and dripping slowly off her chin. She rubbed her eyes.

It was true. In heaven there would be no more crying. Not for Danny. He would be with Jesus.

Emma was not sure whether they would have water chutes and raging rapids in heaven. But if they did, Danny would be able to go on them all. He could snorkel with the beautiful fish, he could swing from ropes, he could run, and jump, and ski. In heaven Danny could somersault, ride his skateboard and never cough. He would not cry.

But she would. Danny would be safe and happy but she would miss him. Miss him terribly. She could not remember a time when he had not been there. And now she knew. The time was coming when he would not be here. Mum had said so, and she would never tell her that if it was not true. Okay, so there would be no more crying in heaven. But here? Here there would be loads.

The door burst open. Danny, wearing his killer whale T-shirt and Emma's black leggings, arched into the room.

'I'm a killer whale. I've seen the killer whales!' He sang at the top of his voice. His arms arched, doing a reasonable impression of a leaping whale. 'Eh, what's up?'

Emma and Mum sprang apart.

'Oh, nothing,' said Mum, 'just getting our energy up for the next round of fun and games. This heat has got me shattered. Emma's just going to have a quick dip to cool off before bed, aren't you?'

'Yes, Mum.' Emma was thankful that Mum had given her the chance to escape and to have some time and space to calm down. In the dark outside, or in the pool, no-one would see her blotched and tear-stained face. She looked such a mess when she cried and was bound to get an eruption of spots as a result.

The silky water, warm and relaxing, soothed her tired body and slowly spread its healing qualities into her shattered mind.

'Oh, Danny,' she murmured. 'Danny. Danny.' Her heart felt too full up for her to know what to say. She wanted to talk to God but could not find the words. This news about Danny really messed up the God equation. A plus B equals C, and she did not even know what A and B were any more.

'Oh, God, Danny,' she said, the words in themselves more effective than any long, drawn-out prayer.

The water rocked her as she lay on Danny's air bed. She wanted to curl up, suck her thumb, be a baby again and be rocked to sleep, all the bad things taken away. But that would not happen.

'Emma Fisher,' she said out loud in the deserted pool. 'You are nearly thirteen, you are in Florida, your brother will not live as long as you,' she stumbled over the words, 'you don't understand it, none of it, but somewhere, there's a better world, where there will be no crying ever.'

She lay there, rocking, the emotions draining out of her body, like water down a plug hole, until all she felt was tired and very sleepy. Showering quickly by the pool, she dried herself and went up to bed.

'I'm okay now, Mum, honest,' she whispered as Mum tucked her up, like she had done when Emma was a little girl. 'I'll be all right.'

Mum sat by her, stroking her damp, tousled curls, not saying a word, until Emma fell fast asleep.

Chapter Thirteen

Over breakfast on Thursday the family had a lively discussion about where to go that day. They wanted to revisit their favourite places and eventually decided to do Epcot in the morning and go to the Magic Kingdom at night, to see the illuminated parade.

'Josh can come,' said Mum. 'See if he's free.'

'And the twins?' asked Danny, who had got on with them well the previous day.

'Can't overload the car,' said Dad, as Emma heaved a sigh of relief. 'I'll tell you what though, I'll try to fix up for us all to do something together tomorrow, the last day.'

Emma hung around while Josh got ready. Angie loaded him down with dollars and warnings about behaving himself.

'Josh,' began Emma, 'today we'll, what I mean is, we'll stay with Danny.'

'But we can go much faster on our own!'

'I know, but today we stay together. We'll do what he wants.'

Josh looked at her but she refused to meet his stare. 'Okay, if that's what you want, it suits me.' He hadn't seen Emma look so stubborn before.

At Epcot Mum wanted to visit the World Showcase area. All around the huge lake were areas made to look like different countries. Mum was insistent that they saw it all.

'But, Mum, I want to go on the computers,' said Danny, 'and get to the Living Seas and go on . . .'

'You can't stay on your own,' said Dad. 'Anyway I'm gasping for a pint of real beer at the English pub.'

'You'll gasp at the prices,' Mum remarked.

'Mum, why don't me and Josh stay with Danny?'

'Emma, you'll argue, or leave him.'

'Mum,' Emma tugged her arm. 'I won't. Honest. Trust me.' She looked hard at Mum and Mum nodded.

'Okay, stay together. Here are his pills if he has a drink. We'll see you at the restaurant, same as last time.' Mum and Dad strolled off, hand in hand, looking relaxed and happy, Mum explaining something to Dad about Emma being old enough.

'Right, Living Seas,' said Josh, grabbing the wheelchair.

Emma stopped him. 'Hang on a minute. What do you want to do, Danny, your choice?'

'The Seas'll do as long as I can come back to the computers later.' Emma pushed him, telling Josh that he was her brother, after all. They dawdled watching the fish. Danny bought loads of postcards of sharks and manatees and Josh had a go at getting into a deep-sea diving suit. He could barely move and looked more like a space man than a diver. He treated them all to Cokes, peeling dollar bills off the wad his mum had given him.

'I'll have a chocolate chip cookie, as well,' said Emma, not wanting to miss the opportunity.

'And one of them fudgy things for me,' called Danny.

Emma steered him expertly to a table. She felt very grown-up and mature, almost proud of the way she could care for her brother. He took his pills with no fuss, thank goodness, and managed a second helping of the fudgy biscuits.

'What's it like in that thing?' asked Josh, banging the arm of the wheelchair.

'Okay,' Danny grinned. 'Tell you what, why don't you have a go?'

'Shift then.'

'Josh, wait until we are outside.' Emma guided the chair onto the wide pathways, installed Danny on a bench and started to push Josh in and out of the tubs of flowers.

'Faster!'

She trotted, then galloped, Josh whooping like a cowboy, twirling his baseball hat round his head. Emma spun him round suddenly, the wheels screeching in protest.

'My turn.' She tipped him out and got in herself. Josh was strong and started to run faster and faster with her. 'Danny! Watch!' she yelled, as she shot past his bench, where Danny was doubled up with laughter.

'Shouldn't be allowed!' said one woman to her friend. They were sitting on Danny's bench.

'That girl's never disabled. Looks as strong as an ox.'

'You'd think someone would stop it.'

The chair screamed to a halt, narrowly missing the woman's feet.

'You ought to watch it,' said her friend. 'Where are your parents?'

'Back at the apartment,' said Josh, truthfully, but with a wicked glint in his eye. 'I've been abandoned, all alone.'

'Cut it out, Josh.' Danny did not want any trouble. 'Hold the chair still, while I get in.'

'Oh, your turn is it?' said the woman, sarcastically. 'And what's wrong with a little boy like you? Nothing, I'm sure.'

'I'm not little! I'm ten!'

'My brother,' said Emma haughtily, switching roles instantly, 'has a lung and digestive disorder that means he has to use a wheelchair. Now, please excuse us, and,' she added scathingly, 'have a nice day.'

'I don't know what two old grumpies are doing here,' said Emma, 'but I think we won't tell Mum and Dad about playing pass the wheelchair. Okay, you two?'

'Course. Now computers!' Danny's hands itched to control the screens. Maybe when they got home, they could save up and get him his own computer, one that painted pictures like this one. When he was poorly, he could play with it for hours.

Josh helped him programme games and told him all about different makes of computer. Of course, he had got one at home. Emma felt a bit left out but did not mind. She felt quite important holding the wheelchair handles.

'Didn't you think to look at the time?' It was Dad. 'Half an hour we've been waiting! I thought I'd find you here. You ought to see the stuff your Mum has bought. How it'll all go in the suitcases, I don't know.'

After lunch they wandered round some more exhibits before returning to the apartment for Danny's physio and rest. Emma opted for the pool.

'Where's your dad?' asked a twin.

'He's got to stay out of the pool. His steel chest is

going rusty.'

The twin gazed at her wide-eyed, silent for ten seconds.

'You need wire wool to get the rust off, like I use for my bike.'

'I'll tell him,' said Emma. 'He's oiling it at the moment.'

'Like a car?'

'Yes.' Darlene and Cindy were stunned by this information and it took them a while to return to their normal state.

'Where are you going later?'

'Disneyworld,' said Emma.

'Can we come?'

'No, but tomorrow, I think our parents are arranging something. Why don't you go and find out the details and write them down?' The twins departed. That should occupy them for a while.

After tea, as the sky was being painted in soft hues of pink and grey, the Fishers got into the car for their last trip to Disneyworld. They re-rode all their favourite rides in the Magic Kingdom and made sure that they were in position well before the illuminated parade.

It had started to rain, warm and wet, but no-one seemed bothered as it was still so hot. The rain was quite welcome and the parade went ahead as usual. Myriad, twinkling lights lit up fantastic floats, the last one stretching back as far as they could see.

'And now, if you look overhead by the castle, you may be able to see Tinkerbell flying through the night sky.'

Everyone craned their necks. The timeless fairy flew above their heads, captured in the spotlight, like a moth in a torch's beam. Emma was delighted. She knew it was really just a woman dressed up, dangling from a strong wire, but it was still magic.

'Fancy putting that on your tax return form,' said Dad, 'in the space marked "Occupation". Flying fairy! The tax people would think you were nuts.'

'Mark, you're spoiling it.'

Dad was well away. 'Or you could put Dancing Dumbo or Magic Mouse, or . . .'

He was interrupted by the first burst of fireworks. Emma stood, her hands resting lightly on the wheelchair in front of her. Cinderella's Castle was lit up in patriotic bands of red, white and blue. Huge flower-shaped fireworks burst open, their petals next to the castle's pinnacles. Flower after flower, each more beautiful, each more spectacular, opened, flourished and faded, until it seemed that there was room for no more in the indigo night. With a final ear-shattering burst the sky lit up.

Danny's face was alive. The glow seemed to have given him an inner fire that burned through his eyes. His hand crept round the chair and found Emma's. She held on to it, tightly, unwilling to let go, even as the sky faded and people began to drift back to the rides.

Could it be true? Could heaven be better than this? It seemed impossible. How could anything be more awe-inspiring than this, the most magic place on earth?

Nearby a toddler fell over, his screams piercingly high. Even in the Magic Kingdom there was crying. And over there, some lad was getting a real telling off from his dad, who looked as if he was about to explode like a firework. Even in the Magic Kingdom there were arguments and grief.

Emma started to push Danny towards his favourite

roller coaster ride. Lost in her thoughts, she collided with another wheelchair. It was an older man, with no legs, who assured her it was not her fault they had crashed. Even in the Magic Kingdom there was pain and disability.

But in that other kingdom, where Jesus was, there was none of this. Maybe, after all, heaven was better than all this, better than anything Emma had ever dreamed of.

Chapter Fourteen

A thunderous knocking woke Emma the next morning.

'Are you folks ready?'

Mum stumbled to the door. Identical grins topped by long brown ponytails looked up at her.

'Grandma say's we're leaving at nine.'

'But it's not seven-thirty yet,' protested Mum, wiping sleep out of her eyes.

'We've had breakfast,' said Cindy, 'but we'll help you with yours. Grandma's making a picnic for us all.'

Somehow Emma's family got ready for their day out at the water theme park despite the help from the twins. Emma rode in Leroy's vast Chevrolet, feeling like a film star, waving to the hire cars that they glided past.

The water park was superb. Mum, Grandma and Leroy all tried to organise them at the same time, resulting in total confusion. Danny was covered in spare towels until all that could be seen of him was his bare feet sticking out by the wheels of the chair.

'Base camp here,' said Mum, wheeling him under a huge sun umbrella. Its shade spread over several tables and chairs and Mum arranged them in a big circle. Angie had insisted on making a picnic as well, so her cool box and all the other assorted bags were stored away.

'Danny,' Emma knelt down by him. 'You won't be, well, like you were at Typhoon Lagoon, kicking up all that fuss to go in the water, will you?'

'Course not.' Danny looked wistful. 'There's a lazy river here. I can go in that.'

'Em, come here a minute. Leroy and I want to try something,' called Dad.

Emma trotted off, returning with them after twenty minutes. She was holding a huge, pink, inflated tube.

'Danny, they pretended I was you, to see if you could do it, and it worked, so they're going to do it with you. Come on.'

'Do what?'

'Just come. Here, let him walk, Dad, slow like.'

At the edge of the main pool, Leroy picked Danny up, his hairy chest tickling Danny's back. He strode into the water, Dad following him with the tube. Dad positioned himself on the tube, put Danny next to him and Leroy sat opposite. Amazingly it did not sink.

'Now what?' said Danny.

'We float. Together, me and Leroy can make sure that you're okay. He's a good swimmer.'

A whistle sounded and the tube began to rock, very gently, then higher and higher it slapped, as the artificial waves flung them up and down. Dad held the ring with one hand, white knuckles clutching a handle, and Danny with the other hand. Leroy did the same.

Danny was sailing, tossed to and fro by a mighty storm raging far out to sea. They were shipwrecked, dying of thirst, no land in sight, marooned on the cruel, ocean waves, in fear of their very lives.

The waves subsided, the tube floated quietly and Danny was back in the water theme park.

'Again!'

'Sure thing. Let's get our stomachs back. Bad as breaking in broncos, this ring.'

'You broke in horses?'

'Sure.' And in the calm stretches between the storms, Leroy told Danny stories from the ranch, until they all decided they were too tired for any more shipwrecks.

Meanwhile Emma, Josh and the twins were riding the chutes. Carrying their mats, they lined up in the hot sun, climbed up the steps and, clinging to the mats, whirled and twirled their way round and round into the plunge pools at the bottom of the chutes. Time after time they had a go, getting more confident with each ride. Angie and Grandad were supposed to be keeping an eye on them but spent all the time chatting.

After eating the first picnic, they went on the lazy river. Grandma was a sight. She got her well-padded bottom stuck in the ring and went floating off with her legs stuck in the air. Grandad tried to run after her but only succeeded in falling over, nearly losing his trunks in the process.

'Grandad! Wait till I tell Grandma,' said Darlene.

'She won't let you come into the water again. Pull your trunks up properly,' added Cindy.

'You sound more like your grandma every day!'

'Well, she told you to buy new ones but you wouldn't listen.'

Grandad chuckled. 'Hey, Mark, give me a hand to deal with these two,' and together they ducked them under the water, managing to make them be quiet for all of three seconds. They were just having a really good water fight when a lifeguard came and told them off. Swimming quickly, they tried to catch up with the others, but eventually gave up and floated along, letting the current carry them where it wanted.

'Eh, I thought it was going rusty,' said a twin.

'Shush,' said her sister. 'We're not supposed to know.'

'Know what, Darlene?' asked Emma's dad.

'About your chest, and I'm Cindy.'

'My chest!'

'Going rusty. The steel ribs, after the war, and everything.'

He chuckled. 'Someone's been having you on. My chest's the same as anyone else's.' He laughed. 'Well, not quite like Sue's!'

'But what about your leg? The hairy, wooden one.'

'Darlene. You don't always want to believe what you hear.'

'So, it's not true?' asked Darlene.

'Course not.'

'Is it not true, then,' said Cindy, 'about Danny? Him being ill a lot?'

Emma's dad stopped laughing and the fun was wiped off his face. 'Unfortunately, that's true.' He sighed. 'Now, who's for the Black Hole?'

Dad insisted on dragging Mum to the top of the huge, enclosed, twisting, turning chute. It was pitch black inside. The assorted children excitedly waited their turns to ride the tubes in pairs. Danny had to sit this one out.

'I must be mad,' said Mum. 'I'm the only woman over thirty in this line-up. All the others are kids, or men who think they are kids!'

'You'll be fine. Can't come all this way and not ride the Black Hole.'

'Yes, I can, Mark.' But it was too late. Emma could hear her mum screaming her head off in the chute and

Dad yelling at her to stop screeching down his ear. Emma and Josh followed them. It was wonderfully terrifying. In the complete darkness they had no way of knowing which way the tube would turn, or when. With a flying leap they landed in the exit pool. Mum was still at it.

'I told you, Mark, never again. It was worse than Space Mountain.'

'Come off it, Sue. Let's go on the Twister.'

'You're mad. I'm off to join Angie. I can't see her putting her life at risk!'

'Too right,' said Josh. 'Your mum's fun, Emma. I wish mine would do things.'

'I wish mine wouldn't,' replied Emma.

Dad took Josh, Emma and the twins to line-up for the Twister, which plummeted earthwards like a firework that had failed to go off. While waiting, Emma practised Spanish. 'Una persona por tubo,' which, according to the instruction board, meant one person at a time.

'Keep legs and arms crossed,' said the guard perched high at the top of the 'tubo', which twisted below him like demented spaghetti.

Emma could see for miles over the flat landscape of Florida. People in the pools looked like models. Hotels and roads were laid out like a toy town. Down below, an awful, long way down, lay the splash pool at the exit to the tube. Emma felt sick.

'I'll race you,' said Josh, as he stood at the entrance to the double tube. Emma was terrified. If only she dared to turn round and walk back down the steps.

Too late! She was off. In the weird, blue light inside the enclosed tube, she started to scream but within seconds was too petrified to continue. She had never felt her body move so fast. Her legs came uncrossed, she tossed up and down the sides of the tube, totally out of control. This was it! She would never survive the ride.

Gasping she shot out of the end of the tube. The force of the water nearly removed her swimming costume with the top ending up over her chin and the lower part nearly cutting her in half.

'That's why you keep your legs crossed!' shouted Josh, as she made herself decent again.

All the activity made them very hungry, so by mid-afternoon they had eaten picnic number two. Leroy and Grandad took Danny off to be shipwrecked some more, and Dad said he would teach them a thing or two about knee-boarding. This was a way of skiing on his knees, while holding onto a rope that pulled him in a circuit round the lake.

That was the theory. Dad never got as far as the first turn. The jerk of the rope toppled him off the board. Like a prize idiot he never thought to let go of the rope, so he was dragged through the water, half on his stomach.

People watching called to him to let go, but the Black Hole and Twister seemed to have made him deaf. Bravely he clung on, getting more battered by the water, until his strength gave way. He toppled like a stone and was rescued by yet another lifeguard, in a boat.

'Your Mark should have been in show business,' said Angie, as she and Mum watched while Dad bowed to the applauding crowd.

'Oh, he'll try anything, Angie.'

'I noticed. Say, Sue,' Angie looked a bit unsure of herself. 'I don't rightly know how to say this. I wasn't kind about Danny when we first met, you know, saying your Emma was like an "only." I'm sorry.'

'It's okay.'

'No, it's not. I was rude.' Angie paused. 'I reckon I did not know how to relate, how to be with him. I was plain ignorant. He's a great little boy.'

'I know,' said Mum, softly. 'I understand.'

'No bad feelings then, Sue?'

Emma's mum hugged her.

'Can anyone join in?' said Dad. 'Did you see me?'

'See you! You're worse than the kids!' Sue laughed at him. 'At least they can stay on board. Why's it always you that has to get rescued?'

Dad tickled her. 'Lazy river for you, my girl. Come on, Angie, let's rescue Leroy from Danny.'

They stayed until the park closed. Ravenously hungry, they all poured into the nearest restaurant and devoured steaks and French fries, which tasted nearly as good as the chips back home.

Full up, worn out and very happy, Emma stumbled into bed. Mum threw things into suitcases while Dad caught up on Danny's physio.

'Happy, Em?'

'Sure thing, Mum.' Emma snuggled down to sleep. The last day. It had been perfect.

Chapter Fifteen

'Why on earth did you buy all this stuff, Sue? We'll never get it in the suitcases.'

'It's presents and souvenirs.'

'Souvenirs! Whose heap of plastic cups are these?'

Emma shot out of bed. 'Dad, they're mine. One from every place we've been to, and a pebble from everywhere.'

Dad sighed. 'Put them in your hand luggage or they'll get squashed.'

'I've packed the presents for my friends,' said Emma, pointing to her overflowing case. The trouble was that there was no fun or anticipation in packing to go home.

'Emma, strip the beds and check the food cupboard.'

'Aw, Mum.'

'Aw, nothing! Then go down to the pool out of the way. I'll send Danny down after his physio. Watch him, okay?'

Emma completed her tasks and slipped down to the pool. The twins were going home in a day's time but Josh would be there another two weeks.

'Won't be the same without you,' he said, diving under her. 'You will write?'

'Course, and send you some photos. Dad's on his

tenth film. Mum says we'll have to save up to have them developed.'

Josh put his hand over her mouth. 'You're starting to sound like the twins.'

'Oh, no!' Emma pretended to be horrified. 'Here they come.' Actually they were quite good fun, if you were deaf.

'Danny's not done yet,' called Cindy. 'Your mum's slapping his back all over the place. Why?'

'She just does,' said Emma.

'Anyway, Grandma says that when you are ready, she's doing you a real American breakfast.'

'Pancakes and waffles.'

'Blueberry muffins.'

'Maple syrup,' added Darlene.

'Great,' said Emma, who was looking forward to Weetabix back home. 'Let's play ball in the water.'

Danny joined them. He sat on the edge, legs dangling in the pool. The air bed was being packed which probably explained the raised voices from the apartment. He was still as thin as ever but had a wonderful dark tan that made Emma look pale by comparison. Her nose had completely peeled and the top of her back felt raw where she had left her T-shirt off yesterday at the water park. Two new spots had appeared, one right between her eyes, and her face looked as if an artist had tried to make golden brown with his paints, and failed.

Josh's family joined them for the late breakfast. Leroy had a huge grin on his weather-beaten face.

'I've just got to tell you folks that this beautiful lady,' he turned to Angie, 'has agreed to be my wife.'

Hugs and backslapping all round.

'And you're all invited to the wedding in Chicago in

the Fall.'

'Fall?' Emma asked Josh.

'Autumn.'

'How do you feel about them?' She pointed to the happy couple.

'It's neat. You know, I don't mind. He's not that bad. Anyway they told me last night and guess what?'

'What?'

'I get to have my own horse when we go to his brother's ranch.'

Emma quietly munched her way through her second muffin. Own horse. Ranch. All invited to Chicago! Well, she had as much chance of flying to the moon as visiting America again. Perhaps Josh could come to England though. Leroy had heaps of money. That was it. Next summer Josh could come and stay at their house. Mind you, Birmingham was no Disneyworld and the single water slide at the local leisure centre would seem pathetic compared with the ones here. Still, Josh could come. They would have great fun, him, her and Danny.

Danny! She glanced at her brother sneaking maple syrup straight from the bottle. Would he be here next summer? Well, would he?

They all exchanged addresses, hugs, tears, and promised to keep in touch. Grandma would send Mum all her best recipes, although Mum was unlikely ever to cook them. Leroy helped Dad to ram the bags into the car. Mum found a pile of fluffy towels in the dryer that she had forgotten and they drove off, waving to their new friends.

'They're so generous, so hospitable,' said Mum. 'I wish we were more like them.'

'We probably are,' said Dad, 'but different. Remember how we got this holiday, eh?'

They all fell silent. Emma felt very sad as the hire car was returned and they got the bus to the airport. For the last time she stood on American soil, the heat wrapping her up in its welcoming arms. She gazed at the blue sky, dotted with clouds, not wanting the moment to end, before stepping through the darkened glass doors into the airport.

The air conditioning made her feel cold. Security men kept them in line. Slowly they shuffled forward, dragging their suitcases with them. At least Danny could sit in comfort in his chair, through passport control and a quick monorail journey to the departure lounge.

'Still over two hours to go,' said Dad. 'I'm going to wander round the shops. Coming, Em?'

Emma followed and spent her last four dollars on a tiny, model killer whale. The posters on the walls all seemed to be saying 'Stay!' 'Don't go!' Fairy tale castles, wonderful rides, majestic palm trees, beautiful, long-legged, white birds, happy, smiling people, all tugged at her, willing her to return to Florida. All the memories crowded back, jostling for position in her mind. She would have to sort them out later, like freezing the frame on a video, but at least they were all there. All her memories forever.

Again they boarded the plane first and were settled in their seats before the other passengers came trooping aboard. What a difference two weeks in Florida had made. Old men with Mickey Mouse hats on, sunburnt children in Disney T-shirts, large stuffed Dumbos and Eeyores popping out of carrier bags, children clutching new toys and one woman with a huge, furry, killer whale that she was desperately trying to pass off as hand luggage.

They taxied to the runway. Once more the powerful engines roared into life, the plane lifted and Emma watched as Florida became smaller and smaller.

'We have some blocks of weather ahead but we will be skirting these,' came the voice of the captain.

Huge, thunderhead clouds loomed around them. Emma watched as lightning streaked down below her. She was higher than the thunderstorm.

'Bet they have to close the water parks,' said Dad, next to her.

Emma would not have minded even being in a closed park. Anything would be better than going back to Birmingham and school on Monday.

Drinks, a meal, a hostess with duty-free goods, a movie to watch. Somehow the flight home seemed to take longer, even though they had not got to refuel.

They all filled in a questionnaire for the holiday company. Emma gave everything top marks. She could find fault with nothing, nothing at all.

'Ladies and gentlemen, it is an exceptionally clear night. We are flying northwards along the American coast. In a few minutes you should be able to see the lights of New York out of the windows on the left-hand side of the plane.'

Emma looked. The sun was setting but unlike any sunset she had ever seen before. As far as she could see bands of red and orange stretched across the sky, mile after mile, every shade and tone imaginable, an artist's dream.

Down below she could just make out a huge wedge of land jutting into the sea. Here and there groups of lights twinkled like a far distant firework display.

She was flying at thirty-seven thousand feet and watching the sun set over New York. Down there are millions of people, thought Emma, living, loving, arguing, laughing, crying, and I'm up here in a long, tin can flying above them. She felt very small, a bit like she had done at the Space Center.

The sunset continued its breathtaking display. It rivalled anything Emma had experienced in the previous two weeks. It's even better than Epcot Illuminations, thought Emma, better than Disneyworld and all the wonderful magical things I've seen.

All those things, well, they were made by man. Someone knew how they worked. Someone pressed the correct buttons and things happened. But this? This sunset was made by God. And it happened, every day, without fail. Sunrise and sunset.

The plane headed out over the Atlantic, the sky dimming, the first stars gleaming, tantalisingly out of reach.

If God made this every day, then perhaps after all, he knew why Danny was disabled. He knew *if* and *when* Danny would die. Surely God had the answers, even though Emma had not. She would never understand her equation, how God could give them the holiday and yet let Danny have CF, but God *did*.

High above the Atlantic Emma talked to the sunset creator, the One who had made the world, including Danny.

'I don't understand. It doesn't make sense, but God,' and Emma held out her hands, palms uppermost, 'I want to give you the equation. You know what A and B equal, what you equal. You can have the equation, it's too hard for me.'

Quietly, without any words, or any intelligible

thoughts, Emma put Danny in God's hands. God could look after him. He could sort out all the questions. She never could.

Emma snuggled next to the window, staring out into the star-spangled sky. All around her passengers dozed but she was determined not to miss a minute of the night flight. The holiday had been fantastic and Emma was coming home a different person. Deep inside she knew that somewhere there was a world more fantastic, more wonderful than the Magic Kingdom. And one day, not so very long away, Danny would be there.

Some other Leopard Books for you to read:

Roughshod Ride
Gail Vinall

Zena and Toni are suspicious about the stable manager but lack proof. Why is Cheri suddenly lame and why does Steve lose his job at the stables? Zena and Toni are up against a clever schemer.

Hawkeye of Paradise Row
The Paradise Row Gang
Hawkeye hits the Jackpot
Veronica Heley

Three books about Toby, Nikki and their friends. They fight neighbourhood crime, help to pull together the kids in the area into a community and tackle the problem of game machine addiction. Three exciting and realistic stories.

Piggy in the Middle
Christine Harris

Gina is embarrassed by her mother's involvement in a publicity campaign to save their local hospital. She wants to support her mother but it may mean losing a friend. Her brother Charlie is also against the campaign, so family loyalties are tested.

Race to Anderloss
Lynette Bishop

Alex enters a race for a place in a space explorer's team. He does not expect to have to face so many hazards and threats on his trek across the Waste Zone to his spaceship. It seems as if someone on the team is playing dirty tricks on the others. By the end of the race Alex has a different view of winning.

Treasure in an Oatmeal Box
Ken Gire

Kim and her twin brother, Kevin, have moved house and have to make new friends. This is easier for Kim than for Kevin, who is mentally handicapped. His best friend is Wiggles, his Labrador dog. He comes to the rescue when a bear attacks Kevin. But it is Kevin's affection for Wiggles which leads, in the end, to a family tragedy.